PAVOR NOCTURNUS

DARK FICTION ANTHOLOGY

VOLUME I

GEOFFREY K. LIU, EDITOR

Parasomnia Press

Is all that we see or seem
But a dream within a dream?

—Edgar Allan Poe

Parasomnia Press
P.O. Box 152
College Park, MD 20741
Chumbawumba

Cover art: 'Horror Forever' courtesy of Logan Knight
Knightman Productions - www.knightmanproductions.com

CONTENTS

INTRODUCTION

Our journey *Into the Corridor* begins with Troy Blackford's masterful flash fiction piece of the same name, and takes us into a world the likes of which we've not quite seen anywhere else. This is *Pavor Nocturnus*, the name of our anthology, as well as the Latin medical term for night terrors, an occurrence in which the sleeper reacts, often violently, to the transition from deep non-REM sleep to a lighter REM sleep in which dreams come forth.

And that, friends, is why we're here, isn't it? To bring forth dreams ... and nightmares?

Welcome, and thank you for joining us, whether you're reading this on some ingenius little electronic doo-dad or holding the actual printed book—a wonderful reading device invented some years ago in which paper is bound together to allow for maximum portability. You'll notice it has no USB ports or SD card slots. The damn thing doesn't even have Wi-Fi. It already has everything loaded in it that it will ever need.

This book is truly an answer to a longtime dream. I've been a horror writer for as long as I can remember. My story is, I'm sure, no different from those of a lot of horror writers: I've considered myself a horror writer ever since the first time I finished a Stephen King novel. It may not be the prolific Mr. King for every horror writer, but it doesn't have to be. I don't think any right-minded writer wakes up one day and just decides to write down nightmares for entertainment. I think we're all pushed into it in some way or another, by some writer or another. Maybe pushed by one, tripped by another, but we're all on that long fall down this deep, dark well, and we love every moment of it.

I still consider myself a writer first, but there's something I love almost as much: working with other writers and artists. The process of writing a story is a solitary one. I've found that the process of putting together a book of short stories is a wonderfully cooperative one, involving writers, editors, artists, and designers.

Here's to the dozen writers featured in this book, who saw fit to graciously answer my e-mails, often written in the dead of night or morning, and likely containing great babbles of random information and ideas. Here's to the amazing cover artist, Logan Knight, whom I stalked on Deviantart.com and convinced to donate this most excellent piece, *Horror Forever*, so that we could wrap our stories in something amazing, creepy, and beautiful. Here's to the good people of the Rustbelt Rewards company, for always answering our panic-stricken questions on design and layout with patience, expertise, and professionalism.

This isn't my book at all; it's *our* book, and always will be. I'm only the ringmaster of some crazy circus, one in which there are, mercifully, no helpless animals abused into performing. Our circus features only sad clowns whose faces are painted happy, whose teeth are sharpened to deadly points, and who want more than anything to scare the children.

They *love* to scare the children.

Geoffrey K. Liu, Editor

INTO THE CORRIDOR

TROY BLACKFORD

A lmost two thousand people are reported missing in this country each day. Most of them turn up within a matter of hours, or perhaps weeks. Around these parts, many of those who have disappeared over the years really are gone—vanished into the Corridor. The wanderers stepped away from their lives and strayed into a wilderness of trees, only to become lost; each called to a place none of them quite knew, yet which felt familiar to them all.

There, they found a door. At least, it's a door on our side. Over here, decades might pass between the departure of one wanderer and the disappearance of the next. However much time may have elapsed here doesn't matter.

They didn't leave together, but they're together now. On the other side of the door, it's all-time. Boundaries and distinctions turn to dust. Whatever separates one era from the next—one location from another leagues away—whatever nameless force gives form meaning and meaning substance, it does not exist beyond the door. Over there, it's everywhere and no place at once.

No one knows when they'll be back. They will, however, return. You'll be able to feel it. When they passed into the Corridor, they were unwoven from our reality. When they return, their existences will re-form: they will uncease, reweave themselves into our world.

It will not be subtle.

When that time might come, or what happens after, none can say. All we know is this: the missing are gone from this plane, having straggled separately through the door, and into the Corridor—into the place where it is all-place, and into a time which is no time at all.

THE TREE MAN

D.W. GILLESPIE

The weather rolled in from the east, strange for this time of year, and reason enough for the mother to rest on the screened back porch and wait for it like a baby bird awaiting her mother. She often held court there when the air grew electric and thick, the scent clean and somehow hopeful. With reverence, she waited for the first drops to fall, robed in terry cloth and beneath that a cotton nightgown, and beneath that nothing but aged, forgotten skin. The horizon grew blue then black then blurred and misty, and still she sat, sipping dark, cheap coffee in silence. Father was away. Their son was somewhere within. Neither held a place in her mind at the moment.

The first blue vein of light splintered the sky, dividing it like a split mirror. An instant later, the sky was rejoined with no trace of the violence it had just witnessed. Just before the drops began to fall, a chill wind drove through the covered patio, as sharp as a splinter of ice between her shoulder blades. She was thinking about how bad this whole scene was turning when another bolt tore down, all but summoned.

The world went white and silent, and she fell from her rattan perch to the planked floor below. Her ears throbbed steadily, and she was certain she was either dying or dead.

"…wassat…?"

The voice that gradually cut through the curtain of confusion was her son's, though he seemed to be speaking through a foot of concrete. She clawed at the arm of her chair, briefly considering that he would help her to her feet before swatting the thought away.

"What was that?" he asked once more as she found her footing.

"Lightning," she answered much louder than normal. "I thought it hit me."

Even as she spoke, her vision returned in splotches, though her ears still throbbed like kettle drums. The phantom light faded, and the world returned before her eyes.

"Damn," her son said, gazing out at the still rainless storm.

Stumbling and surprisingly weak, she stood in the dim light and stared at the scene taking place just off her own porch. Wind tore at both of them, but they were unable just now to look away from the unreal scene. The ancient oak tree that stood at the edge of their endless, gravel drive was aflame. Leaves—dry from the summer heat—roared, spitting pieces of themselves into the wind to be carried away. The son's treehouse, all but forgotten to him now, was burned black in span of a few seconds. A pillar of fire had risen before them, and despite the rain that was sure to come, the mother found herself suddenly afraid.

Fire's coming this way, she thought as she placed her hand protectively on her son's shoulder. He shrugged it away without a word.

The rain clouds above stopped threatening and got on with the business of drenching the world below. The flames licked and hissed and died as quickly as they had been born. Without warning, the wind gusted and turned, snapping a branch from near the top of the old oak. The mother meant to scream, but she never quite had a chance. The ancient limb twisted, floating impossibly for a moment on the upward current before impaling the deck like a spear thrown by God.

* * *

That night was confusion. The mother and son were somehow both spared from the hurtling piece of wood. The shaft shredded the screen door, and somehow darted between mother and son before tearing a three foot hole in the wooden floor of the patio. Even as the storm faded and disappeared, it stood up as straight as a dart hurled by a giant. The son said nothing of this, for he didn't believe in fate or luck or superstition. But the mother—humbled and deeply shaken by what had happened—spent the rest of the night praying. As her husband cursed through gritted teeth, covering the outside of the deck with tarps and securing the porch for the night, she kneeled next to her bed and quietly spoke to the Lord.

* * *

Father saw it first. The next day was clear and hot, and by ten, the rain had burned off. His back was already aching from the night before, and as he surveyed the scene, the dull pain seemed to grow and pulse in anticipation of the day to come. He stood for a while, as he often did in such moments, getting his thoughts in order and figuring the best course of action to set right what nature had so rudely derailed. Soon after, he went to work, clipping the end from the long spar of wood with his chainsaw before dragging it into the back of his truck to haul away. After the blackened piece was loaded, he drove toward the back of their land, glancing up at the skeletal remains of his son's treehouse, the very same he had built with his own two hands. That was when he saw it.

* * *

They gathered around the oak, mother, father, and son, the three of them staring upward at the ruined cleft the lightning had torn in the tree. There, nestled in the blackened crater like a swaddled child, was a small human skeleton. The white arms were wrapped around both elbows, as if shuddering in the cold. The top of the head was still hidden by the tree, as were the feet, but there could be no mistake as to what it was. It was impossible, ludicrous even, and yet there it was.

"How?" said the father, his voice the embodiment of

childlike amazement.

"What is it?" said the mother.

"Are you serious?" he responded. "It's a man."

"But, it's so very small," she said. "It's like … a child."

The man nodded. The entire body was maybe four feet tall, but the proportions were that of an adult.

"Look at the teeth," he said. "See how big they are? Those ain't baby teeth."

The mother glanced at him as he leaned back with his thumbs in the band of his belt. Lord help her, he was enjoying this. She was as awestruck and speechless as she had ever been, and he was behaving like a child with a new toy.

"What do we do?" she asked.

"Nothing," he answered. "Not yet at least. We need some time to think about this. There's an explanation here somewhere, we just need some time to think."

He tried to maintain an air of solemn nobility, like a big game hunter respectfully taking his hat off as he poses with one leg atop the elephant he just blew holes in. Yet for all his respectful bluster, a smile curled up the edges of his mouth so subtly most wouldn't have noticed it. "I'll tell you this, though. If we do this right, there's a whole lot of money here. Nobody's ever seen anything like this. The whole world will want to see it. Want to know what it is. Might as well have hit the damn lottery."

The mother cringed at the thought. There was something here, even she knew it. But she doubted it was the same as hitting the lottery. This little man was put in their path for a reason, just like that spike of wood had spared her and her son for a reason. She didn't pretend to understand His will, but she highly doubted that God's hand was raised for financial reasons.

The father fetched another tarp and nailed it up around the tree, just in case any folks happened by, and even though he knew this was unlikely, there was something to be said for being prepared. Especially in the face of such untapped potential.

It was a long time before the three of them dispersed. There was a long, empty silence as they gazed up at the tarp, wondering about what was hidden just below. In that time that passed, each of them felt something stirring, like whispers down a long, dark hall, like the half-remembered voices of dreams that tell you everything you want to be told. There was opportunity in that voice, and reverence as well. And, for the son, there was something else entirely.

*   *   *

The son was seventeen and preparing to enter his final year of high school, though in the eyes of his mother, he was closer to twelve. At this point in his life, he had never had an actual job, had never worked a day. School would be over soon, but he vehemently opposed college. His father offered to train him to be a mechanic, the closest thing there was to a family trade, and this offer was promptly rejected.

"He has to find himself," his mother said at the time.

"Nobody ever found themselves watching porn on the computer."

She blushed, and pretended not to hear him.

Jobless, listless, and drifting. Those were the facts, the items on the official record, available for all to see. But there was an underside, the part that was hidden from the light of day, hidden from the father. She knew some of the things her son had done, but even she doubted—rightly so—that she knew everything.

It was she who had found the shoebox hidden at the back of his closet when he was thirteen. There were knives in there, some of them brownish red, the color of old blood. There were bones too, old and yellowed and impossible for her to identify for sure. For a long time, she ignored it, pretended she was just being crazy, that she was looking for things that just weren't there. When she did finally confront him, he shrugged.

"I just found them like that. Jesus, don't be so stupid."

She had slapped him before she knew it, and the look of betrayal in his eyes cut her deeper than she could imagine. He didn't look at her for a month, and didn't speak for even longer.

She promised to leave things alone after that, to stop being such a worry-wart as her mom might say. Boys do stupid things, she knew that. If everything they did while alone was plastered on the front page, no one would ever seem sane or normal.

Soon after, he began staying in his treehouse all hours, refusing to respond to calls for dinner or church or anything at all. Against better judgment, she climbed the thin ladder one day while he was away at school. The wooden rungs led from a cool spring day up into a waking, charnal nightmare. The small room was divided into two separate parts. One side was devoted to dead animals. Pelts, skulls, bodies, and unrecognizable pieces, all piled into an obscene shrine. The second half was smut magazines. Dozens, caked with mud and falling apart at the seams. She didn't know where he had found them, but some were twenty years old.

For a long time, she just sat up there in all that filth, all that lung burning stench, crying her eyes out. Then, she climbed down and fetched a handful of garbage bags and a pair of rubber gloves. She cleaned it all out, from top to bottom, knowing the storm of fury and betrayal that was soon to come but carrying on all the same. Several times, she had to stop to hang her head out the tiny window for fresh air to keep from vomiting. She couldn't hide what she had done, and at this point, she didn't know if she wanted to. She dumped it all in a clearing near the back of their property, doused it with kerosene, watched it burn as black, oily smoke rose into the midday sky. As the pile smoldered next to her, she buried the knives other various tools in a shallow grave.

The son climbed off the bus and straight into the tree-house, same as he did every day. Minutes later, he walked inside and threw his backpack down by the door. Not a word was spoken, and based on his reactions, nothing ever happened at all. She kept expecting the hammer to drop, for the dam to burst, but it never did.

As far as she knew, her intervention had fixed the problem, and nothing else needed to be said. The less she knew, the better, in this case. The reality was far worse, however. Her son had been scared after his mother's intrusion, but just enough to hide his activities. She never knew about the eight year old girl down the road. No one except the two of them knew that, and he was so convincing in his promises to her, that it would be a long, long time before she mentioned it to anyone. The blood on the handle of an old screwdriver had been hers, and now, thanks to his mother, the evidence was gone.

* * *

The night after the storm, the son waited until the usual sounds of the house died down. He was always up later than his parents, and this night was no different. He watched some porn on his computer and masturbated, also a nightly occurrence. Around eleven, he shut down his laptop and stepped out into the hall, checking his steps carefully as he made his way outside.

A steady pulse grew in his ears and cheeks as he approached the tree. The world seemed to hum all around him, and for a moment, he swore he heard whispers echoing from behind the blue tarp, beckoning him forward. The thrum grew as he reached up toward the tarp with a feeling of apprehension he had not felt since his time with the girl down the street. He stood bare chested before the tree, shivering in the night, and with a single arm, he tore the covering away.

It was grotesque in the moonlight, but oddly alluring at the same time. His heart smashed against the shell of his ribs, and his eyes burned because he refused to blink them. He felt a sudden urge to strip away the rest of his clothes and stand before the horrible thing, and he did so at once. Naked in the gaze of the tree man, he felt like a child more so than he could ever remember. His body tingled as the empty, black sockets peered over his bare flesh. A trickle of blood ran from one ebony socket and snaked its way down the yellowed cheek bone.

Was it real? The son didn't know, but the world seemed to

shake, and his body ached with some unexplained longing. All at once, he became aware of his own arousal, surprised he hadn't noticed it earlier. He laughed and grabbed himself as a spider walked from the open mouth and crawled downward along the narrow bridge of collarbone.

It was all so real. All of it, like being alive, the immeasurable power of it.

The son was dimly aware that he was pleasuring himself when he noticed the first tickle around his feet. He glanced down and gasped at the sight of uncountable numbers of insects swarming around him. The tree man was holding court here, and all had come to see and listen and stand paralyzed in that gaze. As he climaxed, a voice grew clear in his head, and with a sudden clarity, he knew what was expected of him.

* * *

The father had been a mechanic and part time welder for most of his adult life, but it wasn't his true passion. Most men like him didn't have passions, at least not the way he did. Despite his hands-on trade, he was, deep down, an artist. The ability to create with his hands fueled him in ways that his wife and son could never really understand. She would smile at his works and give him a non-committal, "That's nice honey," but she never truly understood it. That lack of appreciation for what he created did not stifle him however; it drew him in deeper and deeper until his hobby had become a separate life.

Never before had he placed a brush to a palette or strummed his fingers across the strings of a guitar. His medium was the very thing he had spent his life understanding. Few people knew metal the way he did, and few could make it dance like him. Sheet metal, car parts, roofing, whatever he could find became his paint, and in his hands a welding torch became his brush. At first, he created for himself only, barely letting anyone else see his works, including his family. Deep down, he was embarrassed of showing the world what he could do, of what he was. He had a shop at the back of their property, and behind it in an empty field, a garden of metallic life began to grow. In time, it was impossible to hide. When a county tax appraiser noticed the blooming museum and loved what he saw, everything changed.

That first piece, a palm tree made exclusively from car parts, sold for three thousand dollars, and a business was born. Never before had he felt so vindicated, so very free. It was never enough to quit his job, but it made things easier for the family, and it fulfilled him in ways that they never seemed to. Always distant from his loved ones, he suddenly drew himself into the vast well of his work until his shop became his second home, his sculptures a second family.

Within that home, he began to work on what would become his longest, and ultimately unfinished work. It all started around six years ago, just around the time that his son started to change. It was subtle at first, a gradual pulling away that he assumed was natural for boys his age. Before then, there was a comfortable distance between the father and son, an arrangement that felt somehow right despite the lack of intimacy. They didn't talk much more than a sentence, and they never dared to hug. Even so, the boy would watch his father for hours as he changed the oil on the truck, or replaced the water pump on a neighbor's Chevy.

As soon as the boy could walk, he was there, a veritable second shadow to his father, and though he would never say it aloud, pride welled in the old man's chest whenever the boy asked a question he could answer.

When the boy changed and all that ended, the man turned his attention toward a sculpture that would steal years from his life. The sculpture was of a metal man holding a square-headed hammer above his head with a small, incomplete metal boy at his feet. The image was simple and clear. It was capturing the moment of creation, an automaton creating a companion, a father building a son. For years it had grown and changed, always in constant motion like the shifting bed of a river. Days might pass without any work on it, but whenever a spare moment arose, the father would quietly survey and critique the piece, bending a joint here or shaping an edge there.

Only once did his wife mention it after stumbling upon it behind the shop, and the only answer she received was an abrupt, "It's not finished." That had been four years ago, and no one had mentioned it since.

*　*　*

He called out of work and spent most of the following day working on the deck. By dusk, he had things in order as well as he could. He would need to make a trip to the lumber yard to get some supplies, but after a weekend of solid work, the job would be done.

As the sun began to wane overhead, he strolled to the back of his shop. His brow was gritty with dirt and sweat, and his back was aching, but he wanted to spend some time on his project. Just a minute or two was all he needed. Some ideas had come to him throughout the day as he toiled away at the deck. A few minutes would be all it took.

The tarp he kept on the sculpture was off, and for a moment, he suspected that the storm had left damage back here. Then he saw the rusted fence rail sticking out of the sculpture's head. Next to it was his sledgehammer.

The father's face turned red and veins bulged around his eyes. He never screamed, never lost his temper, but standing in the orange light with his shadow stretching behind him, his blood boiled. In the growing shadows, his son stood in the treeline, watching the scene unfold with something like satisfaction.

* * *

When she was a girl, the mother saw something awful. She never talked about it, never really thought about it in any way she could describe. But it was always with her, always behind her eyelids whenever she closed them.

As a girl, she attended a small, old country church for as long as she could remember, and the memories of that place were some of her happiest. Potlucks and singing and praising the Lord, the way that it should be, as her mother would say. She remembered her father as a kind and decent man, but he didn't have much use for church, and despite her mother's protests, she would find herself marrying a very similar man when she grew up.

Other than the occasional spat between her parents, her childhood shined in her memory as if a white veil covered the church and kept the darkness of the outside world at bay. One day when she was six years old, however, that veil was ripped away and torn to shreds.

There were only fragments now, the random pieces that were too complex for a child's hands to assemble. There was the Sunday school teacher, young and beautiful in a way her mother never was, an ideal that a young, country girl couldn't help but idolize. Her mother always tried to put her hair up, to keep her under control, but by the end of Sunday school, it would be down, flowing and waving in a vain attempt to match those golden locks that cascaded down the teacher's shoulders.

Those memories of her were burned forever inside, but she intentionally hid them away, blurred them, changed them. She did this because those perfect memories were so intricately tied to what happened next, forever bonded to a horror beyond her worst imaginings. It was impossible to see one without seeing the other.

She never knew the details. Once, when she was thirteen, she considered asking her mother, but she let the moment pass in silence. The truth was, she didn't want to know. Even shattered into a thousand pieces, it was much too awful. Laying those pieces end to end, finally making that memory whole would be more than she could bear.

There were six of them including her, all between the ages of four and eight. They crowded around the teacher, listening to a story she can't remember. A man came in. They knew each other, that much was clear even to a six year old. He was mad, and he pulled her across the room to talk to her. He showed her something and she began to cry. It was a necklace ... no, a bracelet. Whatever it was, it glittered in the brilliant sunlight that beamed in the windows of the church's lowest level.

All at once, she screamed. So loud in the small room, so painful to tiny ears. There was blood. She never saw the knife, but oh dear God, the blood. Men rushed in, tackled him, stopped him, but she wasn't concerned with that.

Her mother had caught her teacher, was cradling her head, was wrapping her scarf around the hole in her neck. So white, as white as new snow, and then so very red. She came close, wanting to see but not sure why. Both of them were crying, and she began to cry as well. Her mother wrapped her up in her free hand and whispered, "It's okay baby. It's okay."

Later at home, her mother scooped her up into her lap, both of them red-eyed and tired. "You see it now, my sweet girl. You see the world as it is. I'd never choose to show it like that, but things happen for a reason. Now you see the evil that walks among us." She turned her daughter's moon face up toward hers.

"Never forget it."

* * *

Now it was her turn to stand before the tree man. Her husband and son were nowhere to be found, and she felt compelled as she never had in her life. She needed to see it, needed to inspect it and feel it. It was put there by the hand of God, of this there could be little doubt, but she had to know why. Why here, why now, why *her*?

The yellowed bones seemed to glow in the sunlight giving it the look of tarnished gold. The legs folded at the knee and disappeared beneath the charred folds of bark, and something about not seeing the feet made her uneasy in ways she could not explain. There was a sudden urge to touch the bones, followed by an awful, unexplainable intuition that if she did, they would be curiously warm.

Despite this, she felt a certain serenity just by staring at it, and the time slipped away as she stood rapt before it. A calmness she couldn't explain wrapped around her like a warm blanket, and she found herself basking in it, drinking it in like handfuls of cool water. Quite simply, she was held captive by the tree man, and she would have stayed that way for a long time if not for the angry screams of her husband growing in the distance.

She saw him come barreling from behind the house, and heard his curses as he approached with his head down, blind to the world like a bull cut loose from its corral. Even from a distance, she could see the tunnel vision in his eyes as clear as the red streaks on his sweaty face. All at once, he caught sight of her and began storming her way.

"Where is he?" he said, followed by a string of blasphemous cursing. He never took the Lord's name in front of her, not because of his own convictions, but because he knew how she hated it. Now, a floodgate of anger burst and spilled out from his lips, each word burning and shocking her at the same time.

"Who?" she shrieked.

"Who do you think? He ruined it, my sculpture, the one I've worked on for … fuck him, the little ungrateful bastard…."

And on and on he went, growing redder as veins began to rise and throb in his temples.

"Stop it! Stop saying that!"

"Why?" he screamed. "You've always covered for him, always taken his side."

"He's our son!"

She didn't realize he had slapped her for a few seconds. The blow spun her around, and she tottered before dropping to her knees. She looked up at him, his thick fingered hand print on her cheek, his silhouette breaking the dimming light of the sun. They stared at each other like statues, both frozen in the shadow of the tree man.

"He's our son," she echoed, this time in a weak, empty tone.

Still shaking, still fuming, he spat his words out through clenched teeth. "That's not enough anymore."

The mother hung her head and began to slowly rub her aching cheek. Just once she glanced up to see the skeletal face grinning down at her.

* * *

The first thing he did in the house was flip over the small table that sat next to the front door, spilling the vase and flowers that rested there. Next was the picture that hung on the opposite wall, a montage of smiling portraits of the family through the years. It cracked on the carpeted floor, and he stomped it once more just to hear it crunch under his boot. Down the hall he went, snatching pictures off the walls before kicking the bedroom door open. His heart raced, and he felt a sudden rush of cold sweat and an odd tingling in his fingers. He ignored it and swung open the closet door before reaching in for the twelve-gauge shotgun that rested in the corner. It was gone.

Behind him, he heard the unmistakable sound of the gun racking as someone chambered a fresh round. He turned to see his son standing there with the barrel leveled at his father's chest.

"What the hell are you doing?"

The boy smiled. "I could ask you the same. You looking for something?"

"I was just looking for it to…."

"To what? Clean it?"

The father's breath was growing heavier now, and for a brief moment, he swayed a bit to one side before straightening back up.

"Why did you do it?" he pleaded to his boy. "It was all I had."

His son smiled at him, a hungry, hollow smile. "I know. He told me."

The gunshot echoed in the small room, and a plume of smoke burned the son's nose. When the air cleared, he saw his father on his knees as plaster rained down like snowflakes. He had fired above his head on purpose, but the outcome had been the same either way. His father's eyes bulged obscenely as his heart attempted to drive itself from his chest. The heart attack left his mouth gaped open as a deep, horrid wheeze whined out from the bottom of his lungs before thinning out to a barely audible whimper. In a few seconds, there was no sound at all, and the old man fell forward, purple-faced and dead.

The son stood there, an odd smile still clinging to the corners of his mouth. The smile never left his face until he turned to leave and felt the nickel bladed chef's knife plunge into his chest. It didn't hurt much at all. The knife was incredibly sharp, and it slid easily in between two ribs to clip one of the massive veins that ran toward his heart. The son didn't know that, of course. All he knew was that his mother was standing very close to him, so close he could smell her. She smelled like outdoors, like the grass and the warmth of the sun. A look of sorrow and fear painted her face.

"You…," she whimpered. "You made me do this."

"Mom?" he said, his voice weak.

"I knew," she said through her tears. "I always knew what you were."

The sudden drop of blood pressure hit him, and he fell where he stood like a dropped bag of clothes, as if he had been dead for hours. She stared at him, eyes streaming. Both of them were dead; her family was gone just like that, as easy as snapping her fingers. She thought of a day long ago, and a lesson she learned about the terrible speed at which people could leave forever. There was more, something she could remember if she ever wanted to. She didn't.

The tree man invaded her mind, clawing in with bony fingers, and she knew she needed to see it, to stand before it once more and pray, to ask it why. She stumbled, feeling drunk and helpless, toward the back door, steadying herself with her hands as she went. Never before had she been so lost, never before had she felt so alone.

Nightmares have to end, she thought to herself, but as the statement echoed in her mind, it sounded too much like a question.

She heard the footsteps as she passed through the foyer, a small, forgotten sound, but one that never really left her. Like a song on the radio, or the smell of a favorite meal, the sound stirred something heartbreaking inside her. Tiny, bare feet were scuttling along behind her down the hallway. She turned, the chef's knife held before her like a spear, and she saw her five-year-old son round the corner. It wasn't real. The simple fact was that it couldn't be real, and yet, facts meant nothing in the face of such a thing. Time, the greatest thief mankind has ever known, had returned this moment to her, had given back what was so cruelly stolen.

The knife fell uselessly to the floor.

"You dropped it mama," he said. His voice was the sweetest music her ears had ever heard. "I get it," he said with a smile.

He pattered forward, and she spread her hands wide. "Yes baby. Bring it here. Bring it to mama."

"I get it," he said once more.

He spilled into her arms, and she wrapped him up, barely feeling the knife in her belly. It was the smell that brought her back, not the sweet, gentle smell of a child, but a dark odor of sweat and blood. Her son, half a foot taller than her and seventeen once more, leaned into her and spilled onto the floor, too weak to keep up on his feet. His last bit of energy had been well spent, and as he crumpled, the knife still jutted obscenely from her belly.

For a long time, she just stood there, hands out in front of her like a woman who just dropped full mug of coffee and doesn't even know how to start cleaning up. Her eyes were glazing, and her blouse and pants were solid red. There wasn't much time, and she suddenly seemed to realize that.

On wobbly legs, she passed through the front door and stumbled toward the old oak. She couldn't make the last few steps, and was forced to crawl the final ten feet. Then she peered up, gazing at it as the sun finally disappeared. A prayer ran through her head, passing quietly over her lips as she swayed slowly in the twilight. Now, as it was before, she felt compelled to touch it, to use her last moments to prove to herself that this impossible thing was real.

She reached up with both hands, clutching the wood around the feet, feeling desperate because she was too weak to reach any higher. The feet were still hidden behind the charred layers of bark, and she began tearing at it with her nails, chipping and breaking them as she pulled the burnt chunks away. She was dimly aware she was crying once more, and as she grasped a wide piece and tugged with all her remaining strength, a scream escaped from her lips.

The piece fell away, and she raised her eyes one final time. With something like madness she stared at the place where the feet should have been. Attached to the bony ankles were not feet, but hooves, a pair of them, each one cloven down the center. Shaking, she stared up once more at the face that had once seemed angelic and heaven sent. Now, the empty black eyes stared cold and uncaring, and the curled mouth smiled down mockingly.

No more prayer left her lips, and she fell onto her side. In minutes, she was dead, and the last feeling to shadow her mind was not hope, but despair.

* * *

Some time later, the wind blew in and the air grew heavy with the oppressive weight of a sudden summer storm. A light rain began to fall onto the eager ground, and without warning, another bolt of lightning struck the tree and the skeletal remains that rested there. The thin body exploded into thousands of fragments, and the tree once more burst into flames, and by the time the sun rose once again, no trace of the tree man could ever be found.

A Breath From Heaven

A Play in One Act

James Michael Shoberg

Sean Michael Gallaher as "The Broken Angel," courtesy of Heather Gray (2010)

Cast of Characters:

Radio Voice #1 (recorded): The voice of a newscaster.

Radio Voice #2 (recorded): The voice of a newscaster.

Radio Voice #3 (recorded): The voice of a newscaster.

The Voice of Mother: The mother of the baby. She is heard from offstage.

The Broken Angel: The figure of a beautiful, yet tragic young man. He is bare-chested, with his waist wrapped in a long, tattered, bloodstained wrapping. Armored guards protect him from wrist-to-elbow, and armored greaves from knee-to-ankle. His feet are bare. Bone and blackened feathers, the meager remnants of his charred wings, protrude directly from his back (*Suggested costume description. Actual pieces employed are at director's discretion and determined by resource limitations.*)

The Voice of Lucifer: The eldest and most beautiful of all angels. He is heard from offstage.

The Voice of the Holy Man: A man who is addressing his congregation as the Broken Angel listens from high above, while resting upon the roof of a church. The Voice of the Holy Man is heard from offstage.

The Voice of Father: The father of the baby. He is heard from offstage.

**Characters other than the Broken Angel are represented as *voices* and not *physically*, as to establish the air of loneliness and isolation that the he must endure.

SETTING: A baby's nursery, in the evening.

> (Before the lights rise, several news bites
> are heard, cutting from one to another
> through static, as if from a radio.)

RADIO VOICE #1

Sex tourism is a very lucrative industry that spans the globe. Two-to-fourteen percent of the gross domestic product of Indonesia, Malaysia, the Philippines, and Thailand is derived from it, and the most significant societal factor that pushes children into prostitution is…
> (The next voice overlaps.)

RADIO VOICE #2

…after his arrest, police and prosecutors revealed grisly details of the crime, saying the man raped the ten-year-old girl's corpse and planned to eat her flesh. A medical examiner's report released later indicated there were in fact signs of…
> (The next voice overlaps.)

RADIO VOICE #3

…was jailed Monday on a charge of aggravated murder,

more than a year after she brought her dead, month-old baby to a hospital. Bail was set Tuesday at one-million dollars. "We have reason to believe, and we have some forensic evidence that is consistent with our belief, that a microwave oven was used in this death," said the Director of...

> (The radio fades. A phone is heard ringing from offstage, followed by The VOICE OF MOTHER.)

VOICE OF MOTHER

Hi, Mom. Oh, he's doing just fine. I know you were. I was worried too, but the hospital couldn't keep him indefinitely. Mm-hmm, the doctor said that his progress was nothing short of miraculous, and that he was strong enough for us to bring him home. I couldn't wait to show him his new room. You should see him in the crib you bought ... he looks just like a little ... *no*, I can't hold him up to the phone right now. *I'm sorry Mom*, but it took me over an hour to get him to stop fussing. You can talk to him all you want when you see him on Saturday.

> (A soft, yet eerie tune is heard from all around, like that produced by a music box.)

AT RISE: The lights rise to a dim, atmospheric level, on an area containing a baby's crib with a bundle resting inside. A rocking chair sits nearby, covered with a blanket and several stuffed toys. Any other simple nursery furniture or accents can also be added to the scene. After a few moments, the BROKEN ANGEL, a cheerless, yet beautifully statuesque male figure, emerges from the shadows upstage. The light soon reveals the various details of his elaborate armor, his injured wings, and the chains, which bind his wrists and ankles. He slowly approaches the crib and gazes down into it, as the music fades.

BROKEN ANGEL
(Tenderly.)
Try as I might, I simply cannot save them all. So many babes are brought into this world, without a second thought given to the hardships that they will inevitably face … *innocents*, often granted life by those, who are no more than babes themselves. It is a circle of *suffering* … a *circle* that must be broken. That is why I have taken it upon *myself* to grant mercy to the little ones. They should be *spared* from the same evils both *created* and *endured* by their parents.

(The Broken Angel leans over the crib as
his attention shifts to the baby's face.)
'Tis *true*, my love. *His* glory…

(He gives a quick glance skyward and then
returns his attention to the baby.)
…can be seen in the faces of *all* His children, and that *glimpse* is *all* that I have left … my *impetus* … the *light* that has guided me through the ages.

(He runs his hand along the side of the crib
as he moves away from it, and speaks in a
melancholy tone.)
I was once like you…

(He pauses.)
…*a perfect beauty.* I knew not the sensation of *earth* beneath my feet…

(He runs his bare toes across the floor. Once
again, he glances upward.)

…for *I* tread the *clouds*. It was *then* that my now *charred* wings spread wide, and carried me aloft to greet my brothers, and kneel in deference before the Throne of Light.

> (The baby begins to coo. The Broken Angel, whose tone has been brightened by his memories, turns back in elation.)

Yes! I knew not the meaning of *sin* or *iniquity*, only the loving word of The *Father*, who took great pleasure in beholding the splendor of the delicate, winged *jewels*, which adorned His Paradise.

> (He pauses.)

And the *eldest* of us, shone brighter than any other … *no*, he was not merely the *brightest* … he was also the most *beautiful* … *glorious* … *powerful*.

> (Softly.)

Oh, how I loved him … *loved* and *trusted* … how else could I have been so easily influenced, child? There was a time, you see, when my brother was summoned before The Father and charged with the declaration that *all* sons of the sky, *despite* the height of their Order, would be called upon to kneel before His newest creation … *man*. But how could we be expected to hold Heaven's favor for so very long, only to be asked, nay, *commanded*, to step aside?

> (The baby is heard fussing. He returns to the crib's side and speaks in a comforting tone.)

Hush now, little one. I hold no ill will toward your kind. *Quite the contrary.* But you must understand that this decree was no triviality. And thusly, the *brightest*, most *beautiful*, *glorious* and *powerful* among us, the brother I so loved, *Lucifer*, rose to his feet in defiance, and, displaying *no* humility, spoke

boldly and freely…
>   (The Broken Angel looks off into the
>   darkness. The VOICE OF LUCIFER is
>   heard from offstage.)

VOICE OF LUCIFER

Why should a son of *fire* be forced to bow before a son of *clay*?

BROKEN ANGEL
>   (Leaving the crib's side.)
He then removed himself, and when next his wings did fold behind him, he was standing…
>   (The Broken Angel turns his head back in
>   the direction of the crib.)
…before *me*.
>   (He begins to speak in a guilty tone.)
I could not have known his *true* design. His words to me were those of deepest concern, not the ravings of a villain. Lucifer spoke of an angel's undeniable superiority, and his belief that with the full support of the Heavenly Host, he might still sway The Father, and preserve our place in His heart. He called upon *me* to gather those willing to listen.
>   (He becomes more emotional.)
What reason had I to think that he would *deceive* me … that he was using me to create a legion to march against the Throne of Light? Lucifer did not wish to *sway* The Father, but instead to *supplant* Him … crushing *all* who would impede.…
>   (He pauses.)
It was not until he addressed the *others* … the *multitude* of

angels, whom *I* assembled, that his bitter ambition became clear. So *quickly* did he stoke their ire that I…

(He stops and begins again.)

…I could do nothing but look on … as *vanity*, the *sin* born in *Paradise*, spread like a *plague*.

(The sounds of clashing swords and battle
cries resonate beneath his lines.)

The *war* that ensued shook the sky, as, for the *very first time*, angels were acquainted with *agony*. They were cut down … one-by-one … be they archangel, cherubim, seraphim, or virtue. Though blinded by a rain of divine blood, I struggled forth, guided by the Light of The Father.

(The sounds of battle fade.)

And *there*, locked in combat before His throne, I found the two angels closest to my heart … Lucifer … and dear Michael. As Gabriel's horn sounded above the din, Michael disarmed our arrogant brother, and then raised his burning blade in judgment.

(He clutches his fist.)

I could not stand by … I *would* not … while one of these two beauties, the *mightiest* of the *mighty*, vanquished the other. I flew between them and drew my sword to deflect the blow, which had already been set in motion.

(He quickly unsheathes his sword. Its blade
has been shattered.)

How foolish I was to believe that *this* could withstand the stroke of an archangel. Michael's sword shattered it in a brilliant flash, and, had he not stayed his hand, would have cleft not only *myself*, but *Lucifer*, as well.

(He lowers his sword to his side.)

There we lay, conquered, *virtue* upon *archangel* … shadow-

less in the Light of The Father. It was not long after that the kingdom grew still, the clouds now *sanguine* with the blood of the guilty and innocent alike. Lucifer, along with those who acted upon *his* bidding, was expelled from Heaven … plunged into a smoldering pit, an *inferno*, which was to be called *Hell*. The Father commanded him to be content with his prize, for it *was* what he *so coveted*, a *realm* of his *very own*.

> (He returns his sword to its sheath, moves to one of the downstage corners, and pauses.)

He then turned His attention to *me*.

> (He glances upward, and a small area of golden light slowly illuminates him alone.)

As *frightened* as I was, I now wish that I could have *frozen* that moment, for it was the last time that I was to be in the presence of His Light. It was judged that *despite* my *good intentions*, my *ignorance* of *wickedness*, and the *genuine nature* of Lucifer's dark purpose, I could *not* be absolved, for I *chose* to question the *Will of God* … and *that alone*, was enough to prove my guilt. My punishment, however, was far more torturous than that of my elder brother, for *he* did not bear *his* alone. *My lot* was to suffer in *isolation*.

> (He pauses.)

For *my* role in Heaven's insurrection, I was to be expelled no further than the world into which *you* were born. And, when the time of reckoning had arrived, Michael cradled my head in one of his powerful hands, and swept the hair from my eyes…

> (He closes his eyes and brushes back his hair with one hand.)

…with the other. His tears wet my face, as he leaned in close and pressed his lips to mine.

> (He gently touches his lips with his finger
> tips. He slowly opens his eyes.)

Then, unsheathing his sword once again against his brother, he held it aloft, and with it, drew a course of flame, to sear the wings from my back.

> (He stares off into the darkness.)

And I began to *fall* … for what seemed like an eternity…

> (He glances upward into the golden light.)

…the Father's Light fading from view, as my descent quickened.

> (The golden light fades, leaving only the
> atmospheric light of the room.)

Soon after, I found myself *here*, sentenced to *unending solitude*. Neither *seen*, nor *heard*, I could do nothing but *look on*, as mankind evolved, and his *decadence* with him. Evermore, I have glimpsed very little with which one might prove Lucifer's feelings of angelic supremacy to be anything less than justified.

And as the centuries have passed, my despair has grown fathomless. I mourn my *beauty*, my *brethren*, and…

> (He gently reaches back in vain to touch
> one of his absent wings.)

…my *wings* … the blackened bone and feather that serve only to remind. Where once I could raise myself up, without effort, I must now struggle … *climb* … to the top of the occasional church, to listen to an evening service, or to offer prayers of my own … all the while, fighting back the tears of loneliness. But the mortal wisdom, which rises through the rafters, never seems to provide what I seek … *answers*.

I am *always* searching for *answers*. "Why would my brother *betray* me?" "Why was I made to suffer *alone*?" But most of all … "Will I *ever* see the *Light of The Father* again?"

> (His mouth struggles its way into a slight smile and he speaks in a more hopeful tone, as he moves to the downstage corner opposite to the one, which he previously occupied.)

And, it was on *one such night*…

> (He crouches down on his haunches, his toes curled tightly.)

…as I perched high above of a great stone church, that my answer finally came. The night was *cold*…

> (The sound of wind blowing is heard. He wraps his arms around himself.)

…and *spoiled* wings afford no protection from a foe as pitiless as winter. I was desperately trying to find distraction in the sermon echoing below …

> (He lowers his head.)

…but the *wind* … it *bit* with such *ferocity* … *no*…

> (He pauses.)

…*wait* … there was … a growing *warmth*.

> (A small area of red light slowly illuminates him alone.)

A *warmth*, which enveloped me like two immense, loving hands.

> (He begins to raise his head, but does not look up completely.)

No … not *hands*…

> (He looks from side-to-side, with head still partially bowed.)

…wings!
>(He pauses.)

Two … immense … *wings*! But *unblemished*…
>(He reaches with one arm over the opposite
>shoulder and touches his back.)

Their every soft and luminous feather *without flaw*.
>(He looks straight up into the red light and
>reacts with astonishment.)

My Brother! You have *returned* to me!
>(The Voice of Lucifer is heard.)

VOICE OF LUCIFER
Yes, Son of Heaven.

BROKEN ANGEL
(Coldly.)
As a result of my ill-placed faith, fallen prince, I am a "*Son of Heaven*" no longer.

VOICE OF LUCIFER
(Calmly.)
Your contempt for me is well-founded, Brother, but know that I have come to atone for my trespass against you.

BROKEN ANGEL
After time beyond measure, why have you chosen *this moment* to appear unto me?

VOICE OF LUCIFER
It was my disgrace which kept me from you. For *despite* my crime, you still held Michael's blade at bay. How could

I face you, Brother? How could I face you, until I could make amends ... *assist* in sending you *home*?

BROKEN ANGEL
(In disbelief.)

Impossible.

(He comes to his feet.)

This is *God's Will*. Would you have me *defy* Him yet *again*?

VOICE OF LUCIFER

Do you believe that this *singular sentence*, a penalty reserved for *you*, *alone*, was without *purpose*? *My* actions led to *bloodshed*, and thusly, there is no salvation for *me*, but you ... *you* were not cast into the *fire* for your transgression. That must mean that there is still *hope*. And I believe that I have *found it* at long last. *Listen well*, young one...

(The Broken Angel turns his head to the side, as if instructed to do so by the hand of his unseen brother.)

...and *know* your *salvation*.

(The VOICE OF THE HOLY MAN is heard echoing from offstage, but it sounds as if it is rising from the church beneath the Broken Angel.)

VOICE OF THE HOLY MAN

In these trying times, neither the *church*, nor the *Lord*, himself, can be expected to *shield* you from *sin*. That responsibility falls upon *you* ... and *choice* ... *free will* ... is the key. *You*, *all of you*, have the *choice* to resist sin. But as it is not an *easy* choice, it is not a *fashionable* one ... so *instead*, we indulge our *baser* impulses … *violence, hatred, lust* … and leave our children without a proper ideal to which they should aspire. We allow them to stumble blindly in a hostile wilderness, doomed to become *prey* for the *wolves.* If *you* will not help them, then *who*?

> (The Broken Angel turns his head back toward the red light.)

BROKEN ANGEL

I do not understand? What do these words hold for *me*?

> (The Voice of the Holy Man begins again. The Broken Angel quickly turns his head back to listen.)

VOICE OF THE HOLY MAN

Think not of your *own* sins, though your lives may be rife with them! I turn your attention now to *Matthew 7:11*, "If you, then, though you are *evil*, know how to give good gifts to your *children*, how much more will your Father in Heaven give good gifts to those who ask Him?"

VOICE OF LUCIFER

It is my belief that your time here is not a *punishment*, but a *trial*.

> (The Broken Angel turns back to the red light.)

The Father is granting you a chance at redemption. He speaks to you now, Brother. Need you hear your own *name* to know it?

BROKEN ANGEL

It has been *too long*. I would not recognize that name, even if it rumbled from above like thunder.

> (The Voice of the Holy Man begins again. The Broken Angel quickly turns his head back to listen.)

VOICE OF THE HOLY MAN

I see that there *are* some who would brave the discomfort of the winter wind to be here this evening. But curse not the air, *chilled* though it may be, for its significance is *great*. A breath from Heaven, it sustains us all. *Psalms 33:6* ... "By the word of the Lord were the Heavens made; and all the Host of them by the breath of his mouth."

BROKEN ANGEL
> (Taken aback.)

What?

VOICE OF THE HOLY MAN

And by *your* word ... *your* breath ... can the world be changed. It is not *enough* that you breathe *life* into a child ... breathe *love*, as well. And *their* breath, the breath of the *innocent*, will *lift* the *wings* of *angels*.

> (The Broken Angel is frozen, stunned.)

BROKEN ANGEL

It cannot be.

VOICE OF LUCIFER
> (Matter-of-factly.)

You now *know* what you must do. *You* are the one of whom

he has spoken. In all of the time that you have spent on Earth, you have seen no real *redemption* in man. There is *naught* in his heart but iniquity. This *holy man* asks, "Who will save the children?" He is calling to *you*, young one. Allow the *babes* … the *smallest* and most *vulnerable* among The Father's…

> (His voice takes on an air of contempt.)

…*chosen*…

> (He returns to his former, compassionate tone.)

…to relinquish into *your* keeping, the *breath* that you require to restore your wings. And, with *mercy* and *gratitude*, deliver them into *His* arms, where they will know not *pain*. *This* is your *trial* … *and* your *purpose*.

> (The Broken Angel turns back toward the red light.)

Once you have fully healed, you will be *forgiven*, and you may *ascend* once more. I can only pray that the aid, which I now offer, will heal the past, *and* your faith in the condemned, as well.

BROKEN ANGEL
(Elated.)
Yes, beloved. And when the time comes, I shall tell The Father of your selfless act of contrition.

> (The red light begins to fade.)

VOICE OF LUCIFER
Fear not, Brother.

> (His voice takes on a more vengeful tone.)

The part, which *I* have played, will be *apparent*.

(The red light fades gradually, but
completely, leaving only the atmospheric
light of the room. The Broken Angel moves
back to the side of the crib.)

BROKEN ANGEL
(Gently.)
My work may yield many tears, but what I do is for the
greater good. I have brought peace to the innocent. *I* have
spared them the sorrowful lives that have been laid out
before them, for *that* is my *destiny* … a path, which has
never been an easy one. For every child I release, there is a
mother, whose piercing cries of agony I can sense long after
I have taken my leave. But those, who have suffered this
unbearable anguish, have done more than simply serenade
me with their lament. In their benevolence, they have seen
fit to confer upon me a new name, as well … a *name* to
replace the one…
(He glances upward.)
…which I left *behind*…
(He is interrupted by the sound of a phone
ringing offstage, followed by the Voice of
Mother. He listens.)

VOICE OF MOTHER
Hello? Dr. Esposito! How are you? *Good*. Oh, yes … he's
doing much better.
(She laughs.)
It seems as if just about *everybody* has called to check on
him. Mm-hmm, a little while ago. He *was* fussy, but he
seems to be fine now.

(The Broken Angel turns his attention back
to the baby and begins to reach for him.)
Yes … well, I never got a real chance to thank you for everything that you've done for Michael.

(The Broken Angel stops cold at the sound
of the baby's name, Michael.)

BROKEN ANGEL
(Intensely.)
Michael.

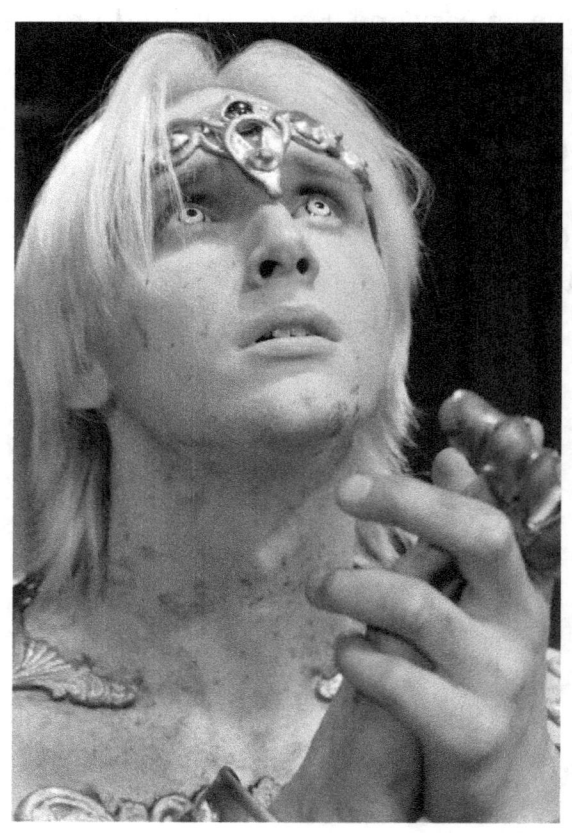

VOICE OF MOTHER

When they told me two years ago that it would be unlikely that I could ever carry a child to term, it broke my heart. I thought that I would die. But if I lost Michael, now that I finally have him, I *know* that I would. He's my joy ... *Jeff's too.*

> (The Broken Angel slowly pulls his hand back.)

And we owe everything to *you.* As weak and fragile as he was, you never gave up on him.

> (She laughs softly to herself.)

I suppose you're *right.* He proved to us that he wasn't so *weak*, after all. Certainly. Yes, next Tuesday. I'll see you then. You too. Thank you for calling.

> (She hangs up the phone. The Broken Angel steps back away from the crib. He glances upward.)

BROKEN ANGEL
> (Confused.)

Another *trial*, Father? Is my brother, Michael, speaking to me now, asking me to spare this child, who beat back death?

> (A door is heard slamming offstage, followed by the VOICE OF FATHER. He is enraged. The Broken Angel begins to turn, as if about to take his leave. He takes a few steps upstage. His back is to the audience.)

VOICE OF FATHER

Lisa! Lisa, where in the hell are you? *Get in here!*

(The Broken Angel stops.)

VOICE OF MOTHER
Jeff, please, calm down. The baby's sleeping. What's wrong? Why are you screami—

VOICE OF FATHER
(Interrupting her.)
Did you hear anything *unusual* today ... let's say, for example, the sound of thousands of tiny droplets of water pattering on the roof? Well ... now I want you to concentrate *really hard*, and picture those very *same* droplets pouring in through the passenger's side window of our car ... a *window*, which was left open ... *again*, Lisa. The seat is completely *soaked through*. How many times have I told you...

VOICE OF MOTHER
(Flustered.)
Honey, I'm sorry. You know that the air conditioner hasn't been working. I must have forgotten to roll the window back up after we came home yester—

VOICE OF FATHER
(Aggressively.)
Goddamnit! I don't care *why*!
(The Broken Angel quickly turns around.)
Do you realize the long hours that I've had to work to provide for this family, which *includes* the medical bills for a sick infant?

VOICE OF MOTHER

(Nervously.)
Of course, I do, but...

                    VOICE OF FATHER
            (Interrupting her mockingly.)
Oh, of course, you do, *but*...
            (He pauses.)
...you still insist on showing me just how *little* you respect
the things we have...

                    VOICE OF MOTHER
Jeff...

                    VOICE OF FATHER
            (Speaking right over her.)
...*especially* those we can't afford to have fixed! I mean ...
I must be on the right track here, because I can't think of
any other reason why you'd make no attempt to roll up a
car window in a *fucking downpour*?

                    VOICE OF MOTHER
I *do* respect the things we have, and I ... I certainly *would*
have gone out, had it...
            (The Voice of the Mother cries out, as she
            is grabbed.)

                    VOICE OF FATHER
            (Coldly.)
What, Lisa? Had it ... *what*?

                    VOICE OF MOTHER

(In pain.)

Jeff … Jeff, *let go*! You're hurting me!

VOICE OF FATHER

Not until I hear you say it. Had it … *what*? *"Crossed your mind?"*

VOICE OF MOTHER

(Frantically.)

Jeff, please!

>(A loud, blunt thump is heard, followed by whimpering.)

VOICE OF FATHER

I'm willing to bet that next time, you'll *double check*, just to be sure.

>(He sighs.)

It's almost time for you to give the baby his medicine.

>(The sobbing continues.)

Get a hold of yourself … Jesus Christ!

>(The Broken Angel returns to the side of the crib and reaches slowly for the baby. He repeats the words of the Voice of the Holy Man.)

BROKEN ANGEL

(With unwavering eyes.)

And by *your* word … *your* breath … can the world be changed. It is not *enough* that you breathe *life* into a child … breathe *love*, as well. And *their* breath, the breath of the *innocent*, will *lift* the *wings* of *angels*.

(He pauses.)

Come with me, dear Michael … for *I*, am the one they call, "*Crib Death*," and *breathless*, you will know not pain.

> (Complete blackout. The sound of a door gently opening is heard in the darkness, followed by The Voice of Mother. She is still trying to compose herself.)

VOICE OF MOTHER

> (Softy.)

Michael … Michael, sweetheart … it's time for your medicine. Will you be a good boy for Mommy and…

> (She pauses.)

Michael?

> (She pauses again.)

Wake up, angel.

> (Her final word, "angel," resonates in a fading echo.)

CURTAIN

END

Passing Through

Adam Millard

The man entered The Scarlett Arms, sodden from the rain and more than a little breathless. As the door closed behind him, the bell hanging above it providing a gentle tinkle, a dozen sets of curious eyes fell upon him. Unaware of the villagers' inquisitiveness, he proceeded to remove his damp coat, which he hung upon a hook beside the well-worn dartboard.

Hushed muttering, which he had previously been unmindful of, caused him to stop and glance around at the faces of those present.

Two men sat next to the roaring log-fire; one smoked a pipe while the other stroked a scruffy-looking Labrador. At another table, sipping furtively from their respective gin-and-tonics, there sat three elderly ladies—no doubt the clucking hens of this particular coup. Open on the table before them was a newspaper with its crossword half solved. The lady entrusted with the trio's pen gnawed frantically on its tip. In a darkened corner, a middle-aged fellow with an abundance of tattoos clung to his much younger female companion as if she was apt to desert him without notice. A game of dominos was being played on a central table, its four competitors obviously irritated by the appearance of some unsolicited stranger. And then there was the landlord, who had been wiping the inside of the same glass since the outsider's arrival.

"Raining," the man said, pointing to the closed door behind him. Quite why he'd made such an obvious statement was beyond him. He nervously wiped his sweaty palms on the front of his woollen jumper and made his way towards the bar.

The landlord, a rustic chap with silver sideburns thick enough to capture an assortment of insects, continued to wipe the inside of the glass, which was almost certainly dry. His left eye twitched as he waited for the stranger to announce his tipple of choice.

"Can I get a large scotch, please?" said the man, drumming his hands along the sticky bar-top. "No ice."

The landlord studiously examined the man for a second, as if he might have encountered him somewhere before, though of course he hadn't. The village wasn't known for its tourists, and those fortunate enough to live there seldom wandered past its boundaries.

The landlord nodded, grunted, tossed the damp towel down onto the mahogany counter. "Anything else?" he asked, plucking a glass from the shelf hanging over the optics.

The stranger scoured the back of the bar for snacks; he was hungry, and couldn't remember the last time he'd eaten a proper meal. "Do you have any rolls? Maybe some soup?"

The landlord stopped pouring and sneered. "We're a pub, son, not a restaurant." There was something deeply unsettling about his tone, though the man refused to allow himself to be disparaged in front of so many people.

"Perhaps some pork scratchings?" he asked. There wasn't a pub in the country that didn't at least offer a bag of something salty and crunchy; it made people drink more, and consequently spend more money.

Slamming the glass of golden liquid onto the counter, the landlord sighed. "I'll go see if we've got any out back." His countenance was one of utmost discomfiture; his gait, as he slunk through the door leading to the back, suggested to the stranger that he might be waiting some time.

The stranger turned to find eyes still upon him. The smoker was prodding tobacco into the barrel of his pipe with a matchstick, though the spilt granules on the table proved he was paying little attention to the task.

Picking up his scotch, the man moved nervously along the bar's edge. Those present returned to their conversations, although he was certain he heard mumblings relating to him. Ignoring them—not wanting to draw attention to himself—the stranger decided to await his pork scratchings without making further eye-contact.

It was then that his eyes fell upon a framed picture, hanging slightly askew, on the wall behind the bar. In it, five men stood proudly before a trophy. The bronze effigy was extremely well done, and in the shape of a giant domino. Without turning, he knew that four of the men depicted in the shot were seated at the table in the centre of the room: The Scarlett Arms Domino Team. The fifth man in the photograph—the one currently absent from the game being played—was easily recognisable from earlier that evening.

"Ah, well played," one of the men said; the sound of dominos clicking together suggested a winner had been determined. "Who's up for another?"

"Shouldn't we wait for Roger?" another voice asked.

"He's not coming *now*," said a third. "You know Roger. That man's a stickler for tardiness. If he's late, it's because he ain't coming."

The stranger listened intently, his eyes firmly affixed to the rotund gentleman staring proudly out from the framed photograph. It would seem that Roger's absence had done little to affect the other players' evenings. *Poor chap*, the stranger thought as he rubbed at the soreness of his wrist.

Just then, the landlord returned with a bag of scratchings, unceremoniously dropping it onto the bar by the till. "That's three pound, altogether," he grunted; his overgrown sideburns came alive as he spoke.

After paying the landlord for the scotch—which was nice—and the scratchings—which were well past a safe date for consumption—the stranger took a seat at the bar and, crunching his way through the packet, listened keenly to the residents of this quaint, little village.

The clucking hens were deciding upon an answer for fourteen down: *Return friends' makeup.*

"Oh, I don't know, Sylvia," the one with the pen dejectedly offered. "We've been stuck on this one for an *hour.*"

"Well, it can't be *that* difficult," Sylvia replied, snatching the pen from her disheartened friend. "It's only got four bleeding letters." She ran the pen along the newspaper, muttering to herself, repeating the clue over and over as if the answer might suddenly, and magically, reveal itself.

"Slap!" the stranger sitting, smugly, at the bar said. All eyes returned to him once more, and for a moment he regretted speaking, though it was impossible, he thought, to keep such an obvious answer to himself while the old dears suffered with utter folly.

"I beg your pardon!" the one called Sylvia said, her mouth wide in an exasperated O.

The stranger nonchalantly sipped at his scotch before explaining. "I'm sorry. How terribly rude of me. The answer you are looking for is, of course, *slap*. Return friend's makeup would suggest the clue to be backwardly cryptic, therefore one would seek a synonym of friend to arrive at an answer. There are a few four-letter alternatives for friend, but the only one which fits suitably is pals, as backwards it spells slap, which is, I believe, a slang-term for makeup." His lips burned from the scotch, yet he mustered a smile that could be considered self-satisfied.

The three women exchanged astonished glances before Sylvia checked the newspaper. "It would appear that our friend at the bar is correct," she said, scrawling excitedly with the pen clenched between her gnarled fingers. When she was done, she thanked the stranger, and added, "Our friend, Elsie, would have got that one. She always gets the ones that are backwards, so she does. Pity she ain't here tonight."

The man at the bar squirmed in his seat and scratched at his wrist. "Could I get another scotch?"

The landlord, who had been watching the exchange

in puzzlement, poured the man another drink. "You're a reg'lar cleverclogs," he said as he placed the glass in front of the stranger.

"Not really," the man replied. "You just have to look outside the box sometimes. Like the lady said, Elsie would've got it."

If curiosity was liable to kill the cat, in that moment it would have slain the landlord where he stood.

The villagers once again went about their pleasant evening, paying no heed to the stranger. In the corner, beside the raging log-fire, the pipe-smoker and his companion were embroiled in a conversation which piqued the stranger's interest.

"So, Albert's coming for Roxy this evening?" the pipe-smoker said, exhaling a plume of blue-grey smoke into the room.

"Well, that's the strange thing," the one stroking the Labrador said. He glanced down at the silver watch hanging from his liveried wrist. "He should have been here half an hour ago to collect her. I told him, I said 'Albert, don't you go bein' late on me. I can't have 'er all night long,' and he promised he'd be here by eight. Now, it's gone 'alf-past and there's no *sign* of him."

The pipe-smoker thoughtfully gnawed at the bit as he considered what could possibly be keeping Albert from his beloved Roxy. "P'rhaps he's waiting for the rain to stop," he finally said. "I mean, it's terrible weather out there, and there's no use in getting drenched to the bone if he knows you're most likely to be here for the duration."

The other man sighed, and stroked the Labrador's head affectionately. "That's prob'ly what it be," he said. "Though

I'll give 'im till nine before using the telephone."

"Give him until nine," the stranger muttered, scratching once again at his wrist and smiling.

"What was that, lad?" the landlord said, his thick eyebrows knitted together with an amalgamation of intrigue and scorn.

"Oh, I was merely considering another scotch," the stranger said. "If you would be so kind?" He pushed the empty glass across the counter, though the stickiness of the bar prevented him from doing so quickly. The landlord, who had been wilfully accommodating since the stranger's arrival, considered the empty glass; the stranger, for a brief moment, believed the landlord was about to refuse him further beverages. It was time, he thought, to announce his departure.

"One for the *road*?" he said, and with a tilt of the head he managed to persuade the landlord.

Fifteen minutes later, with the burn of the scotch still tangible upon his lips, the stranger stood and thanked the bartender for his somewhat reluctant hospitality. He made his way to the dartboard, passing the Labrador owner, who said something under his breath about using the telephone. As he pulled himself into his still-damp coat, and made his way to the door—which tinkled gently as he opened it—the stranger smiled courteously at the villagers. He stepped out into the cold, rainy night, and when the door closed firmly behind him, he rolled the sleeve of his coat up, and that of the sweater beneath, to reveal a row of scars. Twenty-two thin lines, but only three were fresh and already scabbing.

One for Albert.

One for Roger.

And one for Elsie.

The stranger laughed as he made his way from The Scarlett Arms, and as he passed a sign reading OXLEY - 3 MILES, he grinned and said, "It would be rude not to," before continuing along the path.

Sergiane's Choice

Melissa Ferguson

The high-pitched wail of a newborn resounded through the forest. Sergiane clutched the swaddled child to her chest and ran through the dark. Here and there the light of the just-past-full-moon broke through the leaf canopy or reflected off the eyes of some nocturnal forest creature. Leaves tangled in her hair and branches scratched at her cheeks. She stumbled over a raised tree root, threw her weight onto her knees to avoid crushing the child, and slammed into the ground. She stifled a cry and held her breath to listen to the thud of heavy feet and the snapping of twigs not far behind.

Sheer panic had prevented Sergiane from calming the baby before she'd started running; now its cries drew their pursuer toward them. Her knees were bloody and sore and her breath tore through her lungs. She searched for a hiding place. There was a small hollow, just above her head, in a nearby oak.

She touched her fingers to the baby's forehead and whispered, "Calm."

The baby shoved a fist into its mouth, closed its eyes and sucked furiously.

Sergiane placed the baby in the hollow and turned just as Marvel arrived. He stopped and gasped for breath; the knife she'd forced from his hand was still in his shoulder. He grabbed onto a tree to steady himself and smiled at her. It was the same smile she'd seen so many times, a smile that had warmed her heart, a smile that, in the past, she couldn't help but return. Only now it meant something else and the eyes, above the familiar mouth, were different. They weren't the eyes of the Marvel she knew.

"Where's the baby, Sergiane?"

"Marvel, please. She's just a baby."

"She's an abomination. I need to feel her blood on my hands." He shuffled toward her, his hands clasped in front of him, as if pleading. "She's evil, Sergiane. You must feel it too. This is my purpose in life, this is what my nightmares have been telling me. I must end this evil."

She stepped backward and he lunged. His foot caught on the same tree root that had tripped her. He landed on his face and bellowed in pain. Before Marvel could move, she picked up a large moss-covered rock, dropped to her knees, and smashed the back of his head. He grunted, put his hands on the ground, and tried to push himself up. She smashed again and again, until his skull cracked and his wet brains oozed out onto the dirt.

Sergiane dropped the rock, put a hand on the rough bark of the oak and staggered to her feet. She stood for a while, staring at Marvel. His head was a bloody porridge of brain, bone, blood, and hair. She'd killed him. Her man was dead.

* * *

2 years earlier

Sergiane hummed as she swept dirt out of the door of her cottage. The dirt eddied in the wind and settled into the shape of a face. A visitor approached. Goosebumps rose along her arms. She'd been lonely since her mother had died. People stayed away from her isolated home unless they needed something. She heard movement in the forest and leant the broom against the wall. The crunch of leaves and branches grew louder until she saw a strange man emerge.

"Sergiane?" The man strode toward her.

He couldn't have been much older than her own nineteen years. There was nothing exceptional about his appearance; pale skin, brown hair, hazel eyes, average height, and a thin, muscly body. She ushered him into the kitchen and sat across from him.

"You're a stranger to this island."

"Yes. I'm a merchant seaman."

Sergiane nodded. "How can I help you?"

"Townspeople say that you're the woman to see about ailments. My name's Marvel, by the way." He smiled and reached across the table to shake her hand.

That's when it happened. The crooked curve of Marvel's mouth and the crinkles that formed at the edges of his eyes when he smiled made her, for the first time, imagine being close to man. To feel his heat and weight against her. To possess his attention and concern. To not be alone anymore.

Sergiane held onto Marvel's hand for a moment longer. She followed the trail from her hand to his and up his arm to his face. Their eyes met and colour rose to his cheeks. She withdrew her hand.

"So, what has been ailing you, Marvel?"

He sat back and rubbed his hands over his face. "I've been having nightmares. Every night I dream that a great swirling hole opens up in the ocean and the only way to save our ship is to throw a person into the hole. Then all the others—I can't see their faces in the dream—start chasing me. Eventually I'm caught and they toss me in. I'm falling toward the sharp teeth of the world when I wake. It doesn't sound so terrible when I tell it out loud, but I wake up sweating and I'm starting to fear going to sleep at all." He shrugged.

"I'm no interpreter of dreams, Marvel." She liked the shape of his name in her mouth. "But I can make you an amulet to protect you from bad dreams."

"I'd be grateful." Marvel smiled at Sergiane and their eyes locked together again.

"Could you come back tomorrow to collect it?"

"Of course. We're not sailing out for three more days yet. I think I'd like to see you again, before I leave." He looked at his hands and rubbed at an invisible patch of dirt.

She sensed that he had as much experience with women as she'd had with men and decided not to let the opportunity pass.

"Hmm ... perhaps you could give me the afternoon to

prepare your amulet and then return this evening and share a meal with me?" Sergiane's blood rushed noisily through her body and she barely heard his response. She did see him nodding and smiling with reddened cheeks. When he rose he knocked his chair over and hit his head on a pan hanging from the ceiling. She laughed as Marvel rubbed the back of his head. He laughed too.

* * *

Over the next few months Marvel managed to get work crewing ships around the archipelago and spent as much time as he could with Sergiane. Within half-a-year of their first meeting they joined together in a simple ritual to prove their undying love.

Not long after their joining ceremony, Sergiane squatted over the cess-pit in her yard and whistled to a sparrow watching from the roof of the cottage. It had been well over one full moon since her last blood and her breasts were heavy and tracked with blue veins. She hadn't mentioned it to Marvel when he'd last had shore leave; she wanted to be sure. The summer sun warmed her back and she sighed as her full bladder emptied. She wiped herself with a square of moss, glanced down, and saw a dark red smear on the light green. Her hand shook as she folded and wiped again. More blood. She threw the moss into the cess-pit, pulled up her bloomers, and rushed into the cottage. She opened the pantry and pulled out a jar of dried herbs labelled *Bleeding in early pregnancy* in her mother's graceful script.

Fertility issues were a speciality of Sergiane and her mother. She'd prepared this particular blend of chaste tree berries, cramp bark, black haw, partridgeberries, and oat flowers many times. Some miscarriages, she knew, were meant to be—an error in form or composition such that it was a mercy the child wouldn't be born—and some were due to imbalances in the body and upsets of the soul. This tea would only help the latter. She sipped her tea at the kitchen table and lifted her left breast, then her right. They seemed lighter, less pendulous, and no longer ached at her touch. The baby had already left her.

*　*　*

Sergiane fell pregnant four more times after losing the first. After a month or two each tiny life was washed away on a tide of blood. She called upon all her knowledge of midwifery. She altered her diet, brewed special teas, made offerings to the spirits, chanted, prayed, and wore her most powerful fertility amulets in contact with the skin beneath her slip. Even Marvel carried an amulet next to his heart and drank a brew to strengthen his seed. All to no avail.

Marvel suggested they seek help. They first consulted an ancient, shrunken witch on the mainland, renowned for her expertise in fertility issues. They sat in her kitchen holding hands under the table. As she'd expected, the witch's suggestions were remedies and charms Sergiane had already tried.

"Have you consulted the spirits?" The witch touched her fingertips together in front of her face.

Sergiane blushed. "Well, I've tried. I'm not terribly good at it. My mother died before she taught me properly. I need more practise. I can call up faces, but I can't understand what they're saying."

The witch smiled with blackened teeth. "At least that's something I can do for you."

The witch waddled over to a chest on the ground near the hearth and retrieved a little metal box. She ladled water into a shallow bowl and sat back at the table. The witch dipped her index finger into a white pearlescent powder in the box, brought her finger to her nostril, and inhaled. Within moments the pupils of her pale blue eyes expanded until her eyes were black. The witch rocked back and forth and stared into the bowl while murmuring under her breath. Sergiane and Marvel sat still and watched until the woman came out of her trance several minutes later.

"I'm afraid it's not good news, my dear." She reached over to touch Sergiane's hand.

She pulled her hand away. "What do you mean?"

"You aren't meant to bear children. The spirits warn that it could be disastrous to even try."

After that Marvel told her to let it go. He didn't mind not having a child; he only wanted her. Sergiane wouldn't accept their childlessness. She'd come from a long, unbroken line of healers and had always envisioned passing her knowledge on to a young, auburn-haired version of herself. She knew there were magical forces in the world greater even than nature. You just needed to know how to wield them. She'd heard of another witch with a reputation for dabbling in dark and forbidden magic. She met with her in secret. The woman gave her a grimoire and showed her the appropriate ritual. Sergiane studied the ritual, packed a deer-skin bag with the items required, and mentioned nothing to Marvel.

* * *

Several months later, while Marvel was away at sea, she stood in the kitchen mortaring leaves to replenish her jar of anti-impotence powder. She felt a gush from her vagina, clenched her thighs together, and stumbled back to sit on a kitchen chair. She'd carried the baby for almost six months. Her belly had started to round and her hair had grown shinier and fuller. It was the longest she'd carried a child and she'd hoped the ritual wouldn't be required after all. Her womb spasmed and the life within her waned. She needed to wait until the full moon, two nights away, to perform the ritual. She lay on her bed for two days and used all her power to keep the tiny heart inside her beating.

Once the moon rose on the second night she collected the deer-skin bag and put her pet rabbit, George, in a small cage. George had been her mother's present to her on her tenth birthday. Blood trickled down her thighs as she walked through the forest to the dandelion field.

The dandelion field was situated on ley line—a place of great magic where the skin between the worlds is thin. She closed her eyes, held her palms out, and wandered through the knee-deep dandelions searching for a concentration of power. She arranged a circle of stones around a spot where pure magic geysered up through a crack in the fabric of the world and sat cross-legged within the circle. From within the deer-skin bag she produced the grimoire, a candle, a vial of seawater, and a bronze dagger. She touched the wick of the candle with the tip of her finger and said, "Alight." The wick burst into flame. She wet her finger with the seawater and drew a vertical line in the middle of her forehead. Beside that she placed a smear of dirt. She put one hand on the grimoire. It snapped open to the ritual.

"I Sergiane, harness the power of soil, wind, fire, water, hearts-blood, and magic to restore and return that which nature has claimed."

Electricity charged the atmosphere. Her auburn plait rose into the air. A high-pitched buzzing filled her ears. She took George out of the cage and held him by the neck with one hand. With her other hand she grabbed the dagger and plunged it into the rabbit's chest. She cut the beating heart, no bigger than a strawberry, out of the rabbit and placed it in her mouth. It slid down her throat, warm and slippery. She clenched her jaw to suppress a retch. Sergiane plucked a dandelion puff-ball from the ground beside her. The world disappeared. She sat in complete silence at the centre of the darkness.

"Child inside me, I wish for your return and restoration to what you once were and what you should be." She blew on the seed head. Dandelion seeds swirled in the air. Power from deep in the world's core surged through her, like magma through a volcano, and brought life back to her womb.

* * *

After the ritual Sergiane carried the child to full term. As the birth became imminent Marvel stayed with her.

The child arrived in the early hours one morning—with brown hair, like her father, not the auburn hair Sergiane had always imagined. The moment the baby exited her watery cocoon she had an effect on Marvel. As though the life the child had gained unnaturally was being sucked from him and draining him of every ounce of happiness and goodness. It had begun with scowls and angry mutters under his breath. Within a day of the child's birth Marvel picked up the kitchen knife with the intention of killing her.

*   *   *

The baby slept on as Sergiane lifted her from the tree hollow. The forest was silent except for the rustle of leaves and the creak of wood bending in the wind. The forest animals had been silenced by the brutality.

The baby resumed wailing as they approached the cottage. Sergiane knew another calming spell wouldn't work and neither would walking around rocking and singing lullabies. Milk trickled from her breasts. The child had repeatedly refused to suckle, latching on well and then turning her head and spitting out the thin white liquid. Sergiane tried one more time. The effort only incensed the baby further. She suspected the child hungered for something else. She placed the red-faced baby in her wicker bassinet and picked up a square of muslin. From the back of the cottage she collected a shovel and headed back into the forest, towards Marvel's corpse and away from the baby's relentless cries.

With a heave and a burst of power from within, she rolled Marvel onto his back. A sharp waft of stale sweat rose from his body. The knife was slippery with blood. She laboured to pull it out of his shoulder. Once it was out she sat back on her haunches to catch her breath before leaning over Marvel and opening his shirt, button by button. She tried not to look at his face and kept her eyes on the black hairs which circled his nipples and the inked pictures which adorned his skin. Above his heart, a big-breasted mermaid with *Sergiane* inscribed underneath gazed at her. She sobbed and remembered the times she'd rested her head against his chest as she drove the knife into his flesh and cut a deep gash. She found his cooling heart, used the knife to sever it from the attached blood vessels, and wrapped it in the muslin square. Sergiane put the heart on the ground between the roots of the oak that had tripped them both, sheltered the baby and witnessed the passing of Marvel's life. She picked up the shovel and began to dig. She could have used magic, but she wanted to feel the blisters form on her fingers and her muscles ache with effort. She wanted to be sore for days to come, as a tribute to Marvel.

The black fabric of the sky had faded to grey and the stars were winking closed when Sergiane returned to the cottage, filthy, thirsty, hungry, and exhausted. She didn't know which need to attend to first and barely had the strength for any of them. Her child's insistent need roused her. First she would prepare the heart.

She packed wool into her ears, fed the fire, and put a kettle of water on to boil. The baby's cries pulsed dully through the wool. Sergiane unwrapped the heart, laid it on a wooden board, and chopped it. Once the water was bubbling she poured just enough to cover the minced heart and left it in a bowl to cool. She mixed the rest of the hot water with cool water, stripped off her soiled dress, and scrubbed away the blood and dirt to reveal fair skin, covered in light brown freckles. No man would touch her skin ever again. Marvel had died so that the baby could live. He was gone. *Unless* … no her affair with dark magic had ended.

Sergiane ate a hunk of bread and poured herself a mug

of tea while the heart-broth cooled. She poured the chunky, black liquid into the square of muslin and tied it in a knot at the top. She squeezed out the excess and held the muslin to the screaming mouth. The child began to suck and her whole body relaxed, rocked every few minutes by a spasm of her agitated diaphragm. Soon the spasms eased and the baby's skin faded from purple-red to a pink-tinged ivory. Once the child had stilled Sergiane unwrapped her and removed a red-stained cloth from her chest. The hasty healing spell she'd cast as they ran from Marvel had done no more than hasten the clotting of blood around the wound. She'd apply a poultice tomorrow. The child would always bear a scar from her left collarbone to under her right breast as evidence of her father's attempt to end her life. Sergiane pulled the wool from her ears and lifted the sucking baby out of the cot. She inhaled the yeasty scent of the child's scalp and lowered herself into the armchair by the fire. She held the baby tight against her to ease the pressure in her leaking breasts and listened to the awakening birds and the crackling fire. Finally Sergiane closed her eyes and hoped the life she had chosen to save was the right one.

THE SLEEPER WAKES

BRENT ABELL

Darrin awoke and rubbed his sore, puffy eyes. Something seemed different; the vast nothing he had seen every waking hour for the last six years was gone. Instead, light peeked in around the edges of his sight. Color slowly seeped in and continued to replace the black. His father had promised him a cure every day since he went blind and today Darrin thought he had finally succeeded.

Three days ago, his father brought him the first dose of something he'd been developing at work. Drinking the vile smelling liquid brought results; at first he saw light, but the bright orbs quickly faded away within a few precious minutes. He told his father and they ran some quick tests to verify what was happening. His sight returned to complete darkness until his father gave him a larger dose before leaving for the lab early in the morning. Darrin hoped his father would live up to the promise he had made, to help him see again and leave the darkness behind forever. He crawled back into bed and pulled the covers up over his head, hoping for a miracle when he awoke again.

After tossing and turning for a few hours following the second dose, Darrin woke up and began to blink repeatedly, gradually clearing his vision and bringing the world into cloudy focus. Shapes and hues sharpened until, after six years of darkness, Darrin saw images again. His sight was pretty much how he remembered it, except for a black speck in the center of his vision. He closed his eyes rapidly to make it go away, but it remained, hovering in front of him.

He leaned his head back and squeezed his eyes shut tightly. He kept them closed for a few minutes. Cautiously reopening them, he saw that the spot remained and had grown in diameter. Swinging his head back and forth, he tried to shake free of the spot, but it stayed in the middle of his vision no matter how fast and hard he turned his head.

Closing his eyes again and trying to make the black place go away brought with it a new problem: a droning that echoed in his brain. He tried opening his eyes to see if it would stop, but the sound only grew louder. He focused on the noise and it reminded him of chanting. He screamed, his knees gave out beneath him, and he fell to the floor. Curling up into a ball, Darrin whimpered in agony while waves of pain crashed in his head. He closed his eyes again and prayed his father would hurry home.

* * *

"John, I gave the M1-28 to Darrin."

Edward James reached over, grabbed John Clark by his lab coat, and pulled him closer.

"You did what?" His hushed tone was pointed and hostile.

"You of all people know I would do anything for Darrin and I couldn't wait for the okay to start trials in human subjects."

"I know, but your own son? Jesus Christ, what the hell were you thinking? Did you even consider the possible side-effects? Even if the M1 did work and gave Darrin his eyesight back, the method you used jeopardizes the whole thing! The FDA will crucify us, and wait until the media and markets catch wind of it! We'll be ruined!" Edward exclaimed as he pulled John toward his office door.

"Edward, listen to me … it works," John stated as the two doctors stepped inside Edward's office.

"What do you mean it works?" Edward asked as he sat down behind his desk and settled into his posh leather chair.

"Darrin has macular regeneration in his eyes. The first dose only produced a short-lived frame of sight. Once the drug cycled through his system, the blindness returned. After the second dose, a few hours later he came back down from his room and told me he could make out points of light in his vision, which is impossible with his condition. I didn't believe him at first, but when I moved my hands in front of his face, his eyes followed my hand. That was this morning before I left to come here."

"Have you told anyone else?"

"No, why the hell would I do that? You're my partner and we developed that drug together."

"You have to bring him in for me to examine. I need to

see for myself, because if what you claim is true, we've got to study the effects on him."

"What, Edward, you don't believe me?"

"No, no, I do, but I just have to make absolutely sure what you're telling me is what happened before we decide how to proceed with the findings and how we're going to break it to the FDA when they inquire about the unauthorized trial you performed on Darrin."

"Proceed?"

"Yes. How the hell would it look if we just stepped out announcing a drug that cures blindness and that we happened to test it on your son before human trials were approved by the FDA? If we don't get our story straight, we might go to prison. You're my friend and the best damned researcher I've ever worked with, but I'm not going to jail for you."

The two men stared at each other from across the desk. John was surprised by Edward's reluctance to going public and Edward was just as surprised by John's recklessness. They had been partners for fifteen years; the last six on the project started when a four-year-old Darrin lost his sight to aggressive macular degeneration. John had thrown his career on the line to work on a drug that would allow his son to see again.

"How many doses did you administer again?"

"It only took two doses before he started exhibiting regeneration."

"Bring him in now and don't say anything to anybody. If he really can see, tell him to fake still being blind. If too many people see him strolling through looking at things, some uncomfortable questions might be raised a little early."

John stood up and started to walk out. He turned around

and looked at Edward. "I'll get him in here in a few hours, so have the lab ready."

Edward leaned back in his chair and smiled. "Let's see what we have here and then decide how we continue. Be back here in two hours. I'll sign the lab crew out and we should have it without interruption for the rest of the day."

John gave one last nod and walked out.

* * *

Darrin sat in his chair, trembling. The searing pain had subsided, but he still felt the dull throbbing in his skull. He saw things again; it was not the black nothing he'd been cursed with since the sickness, but he saw images. Everything he remembered about his vision, however, didn't include the small black dot in the middle of his sight line. It still hovered in the center of everything he tried to look at. When he moved his head, it moved. If he closed his eyes, it disappeared, but came back as soon as he opened them again.

Years without sight had given him some reservations about the spot, and he wondered if it would just go away. Rubbing his eyes again, he squinted, trying to focus on the curtains over his windows. The bright red fabric still contained the black in the middle. It seemed different to Darrin. In fact, he thought it looked bigger than it did earlier that morning.

A digital camera sat on his desk, taunting him. His father had left it in case he felt like snapping a few frames of his world, trophies of his returned sight.

I wonder if the spot shows up in pictures, Darrin thought, his fingers brushing up and down the camera's side. Without thinking, he picked it up and quickly snapped a shot of the wall in front of him. He inspected the screen closely, but did not see the spot in the frame. To his chagrin, it remained only in his normal sight. Staring at the view screen, a low rumble filled his head.

Since he had gone back to sleep, the static noise in his head had grown louder. Mostly it sounded like an off-air television station with occasional gibberish words slipped in. The longer it went on, the more and more like chanting it became.

The sun began to descend, and he sat gazing out the window. Every moment the spot grew until it covered Mr. Nelson's house next door. The edges were hazy, and he couldn't focus anymore. Most of his central vision was now like an eclipse. The pounding in his head grew louder and now he knew the sounds were chants. Nothing he heard in his mind made any sense. The words sounded like the Latin he'd heard at Mass, but the vibe they gave off was ... different. He tried to block them out, but nothing worked, even when he jammed his fingers in his ears.

Darrin did the only thing that seemed to help keep the spot from growing: He closed his eyes and waited.

* * *

"Darrin? Darrin? I'm home!" John called out when he opened the door.

"Dad, up here in my room!" Pain and fear filled his voice.

John tossed his coat on the stair railing and ran up to Darrin's room, his mind racing about the drug and the fear he heard in Darrin's voice. A gnawing sensation hit him in the gut.

What if there were side-effects? Is he hurt? Does he know I did it because I love him?

The last thought hurt the most. John hoped his son loved him and knew if something went wrong, it was only because he wanted to help him at any cost.

But what was the cost, John? he heard Edward's voice say in his head.

Swinging open the door, his heart sank at the sight of his son lying on the floor, curled into a fetal ball. Darrin looked up, and John could make out the red streaks on his cheeks from his tears.

"You okay buddy?" John asked, kneeling down next to Darrin.

"I can still see, Dad, but the spot blocks most of it."

"What spot?"

"When I open my eyes all I can see is a big black dot and it's growing bigger. My head hurts really bad, too."

"Well, we're going to go see what we can do about it, okay? Let me leave your mother a note and then I'm taking you to the lab," John said.

"Will Uncle Edward be there?"

"Yep, but we need to hurry," John answered, scooping Darrin off the floor.

Hurrying out to the car, John did not notice that Darrin kept his eyes closed and mouthed the word *'sleeper'* over and over again.

*   *   *

Edward already sat in the lab with their assistant, Tony Gallardo, by the time they arrived. Both sported lab coats and were setting up the CAT scan system, running equipment tests.

"John, Darrin, how are you?" asked Tony.

"I'm not too good, Mr. Gallardo," muttered Darrin.

Tony patted him on the head and tried to calm him down. "You know what we're going to do, right sport?"

"Dad just said you guys were going to help me."

Edward stepped over and took Darrin by the shoulders. "We need to look at your brain and see what's going on in there. Once we see what your brain is up to, we can figure out how to help."

"Are you ready, big guy?" John asked.

"Yeah, I am," Darrin said and bounded into his father's arms. Father and son embraced, and then Tony lead him into the examination room.

* * *

Tony finished preparing Darrin for the scanner and then stepped back. He gave a thumbs-up to John and Edward in the control room, and he heard the hum of the scanner. Backing away, he sat in the secondary control room and finished powering up the machine.

Darrin lay on the table and kept his eyes tightly shut. He tried with everything he had to keep them shut so the spot would stop growing. It consumed almost all of his vision. The table he was on began to shift and he grew fearful again. In his head, the chanting for the *Sleeper* drowned out the whir and whining as the gears slid him into the cavernous scan tube.

His father's soothing voice called out to him from the outside. "Darrin, we only need a few shots. I need you to relax, breathe easy, and hold still so we can get a good set of readings."

Releasing the breath he'd been holding since the machine started humming around him, he relaxed. The sounds from the machine did little to drown out the chants. The voices grew louder and pounded in his skull like the beating of a drum.

"Dad! The voices are getting louder and they hurt!" Darrin cried out from the scanner.

In the control room, John reached over and pressed the intercom button. "Darrin, please relax and take steady breaths. We're starting to get the first readings now."

"John, look at this," Edward said, pointing to the black and white readout of Darrin's brain.

John looked and felt his jaw drop. The brain scan highlighted over-stimulated areas within Darrin's brain. The most activity occurred in the frontal lobe. The other data showed increased neuro-activity spiking off the charts. Both men stood, trying to make sense of what they were looking at.

"What have I done?" John muttered, covering his mouth with his hand.

"John, we've got to finish this; tell him to open his eyes. I want to see how the optical signals from his eyes affect his brain wave patterns."

"What are you thinking?"

"I think the M1-28 might have unintentionally unlocked dormant sections of his consciousness that humans don't normally use. Whatever the M1 did for his vision, it also did for his higher brain functions." He leaned closer to John. "Finish it."

The knot tightened John's stomach. His desire to help his son had blinded him to any consequences. Before he decided to use the M1 on Darrin, he poured over the animal trial results for weeks and found nothing that foresaw what appeared on the screen.

"Darrin, son, I know you're scared, but I need you to open your eyes."

"Dad?" Darrin's voice quivered on the edge of tears.

"Please, only for a few moments and then we'll have all the data we'll need to work with."

Darrin inhaled deeply and did the one thing he'd feared all day. He opened his eyes wide.

* * *

The lab windows began rattling, and the lights dimmed and brightened. The scanner's instruments hummed loudly and the glass screens exploded. The room's lights glowed like a sun, then popped out with a sound like gunshots. The men felt the floor shudder and the building quake. With one last push, the lights went out, leaving them in total darkness.

"Everyone stay put! The emergency lights will kick on in a moment. Tony, I want you to get Darrin when we can see again," Edward shouted.

John could hear the whimpers from his son.

"I'm going to get him. I've got the screen light from my phone to help me find my way," Tony yelled.

"Be careful," John answered, and stood to see Tony moving slowly through the room.

When Tony neared the scanner, his phone died out, and then, in the pitch black, he screamed. His agonizing shriek ceased when the emergency lights came on and lit up the room. The dim lights shone on Tony's body floating six feet above the floor. John glanced at the tile beneath Tony's feet, then watched as his head rolled toward the control room glass. Blood poured from the torn flesh around his neck and flowed like a river down his chest to the floor.

John and Edward stared in horror. Another ripping sound filled the air and both of Tony's arms flew and smacked against the window in front of them, splashing gore and chunks of meat on the glass. The bits slid down, leaving slimy crimson trails of sinew and blood behind.

John shook off the shock and yelled at Darrin, "Shut them now! Shut your eyes!"

He could barely make out Darrin's shape in the scanner, but he saw movement. In front of his eyes, Tony's floating body folded in on itself and cracked as his flesh and bones crushed like wadded paper until his remains vanished into nothing.

John frantically kicked the chairs from in front of the glass window and began pounding his fist against it.

* * *

Darrin gazed out into the spot and watched the gray-ish-green appendages emerge from it and reach out into the world. He thought he heard his father yelling at him, but he couldn't make out the words. All he heard was the steady calling of the spot.

"*Sleeper, Sleeper, Sleeper,*" it repeated over and over.

Realizing he had to stop it, he tried to close his eyes. His eyelids held firm, the thrashing tentacles preventing them from closing. Sitting up, he looked at the control room and saw his father slamming his fists into the glass.

Quickly, he wormed his way out of the scanner and looked around. The black hole in his vision consumed almost all of his sight, leaving him nearly blind again. On the periphery, he glimpsed his father and Edward both beating on the glass, mouthing something to him. He focused, trying to make out their words, but they were muffled by the thick safety glass and the noise in his head.

The tentacles battered everything in their path, reducing the examination equipment into twisted, smoking hunks of metal. They tore through everything and the building began to shake violently again. The emergency lights flickered, and Darrin covered his eyes with his hands. He heard the strange limbs still destroying the lab and ripping into the ceiling. Pointless, he dropped his hands down and started lumbering toward the control room.

*　*　*

John and Edward stood in shock. Something crashed through the lab, but they didn't see anything except the dents magically appearing in the machines and the fixtures ripped free of the floor by an invisible force. A loud thumping sounded and cracks spread throughout the thick glass. Looking out through the white and blue sparks arcing through the room, they saw Darrin slowly approach them.

Another loud crash filled the room, and parts of the glass gave out and slammed to the floor.

"John, you have to get him to stop!" Edward shouted over the cacophony.

"I don't think he can Edward! Whatever it is, he can't control it!" John screamed back.

The window burst like a dam and the men were showered in glass. Shards flew and pierced their arms and faces, slicing them to the bone. They cried out from the cuts digging in their flesh.

Edward got to his feet and ran toward the door, but he felt something grab his ankle. Looking down, he didn't see anything, and he tugged his leg. His leg yanked out from beneath him and he crashed to the floor. His breath escaped him and he laid there panting, trying to get air to his lungs for one last chance at escape. Rolling onto his stomach, Edward began crawling to the door. The quaking caused the door to fall over, but any way to freedom worked, so he moved forward. A swift tug halted him and he felt the thing around his ankle constrict. Before he could try again, he felt himself flung off the floor and hovering in the air.

John reached out for Edward when the man began to slam into the hard tile floor again and again. The first few times, John heard the crunching of bones, and by the time he'd counted to ten, it sounded like a ball of ground beef being thrown against a brick wall. Trying to be quiet, John retreated back under the desk while Edward disappeared into nothingness.

Darrin stepped through the broken glass and looked down at his father. Trying to close his eyes one last time, he wanted stop the tentacles from latching on to his father and devouring him into the void.

Then Darrin had an idea.

Olivia rushed in the front door expecting to see her husband and son excited to see her back. Instead she found the house empty and a note taped to the mirror next to the door. Hope swelled in her heart as she finished the note. She ran back to the car.

Her trip to the James Pharmaceuticals complex sped by. In her rear view, sirens wailed and she pulled over to let the emergency vehicles pass. Above her, she heard the whirring of helicopters and wondered what the emergency was. Her foot pressed down harder on the accelerator. A sense of dread filled her the closer she came to the complex. The flashing blue and red lights illuminated the night sky in the direction of her husband's lab. Speeding up, Olivia shot off down the road to her family.

Her fear was justified. Pulling to the guard shack, she could see all the police, sheriffs, and ambulances in front of the crumbling building. The right wing of the building had collapsed and the sparking electricity lit up the night. News helicopters circled the area, flooding the ground with spotlights.

A cop stopped her when she pulled toward the parking lot.

"Excuse me miss, this is an emergency situation and I'm going to have to ask you to leave please."

"But my husband, my son," she started before she burst into tears.

"How old is your son?"

"He's ten and his name is Darrin," she answered between

sniffles.

"Please, come with me now," he said and started speaking into his radio.

Olivia climbed from the Volvo and the officer quickly led her through the commotion to an ambulance off to the right. The rear doors were open, and two paramedics were working around the loaded gurney. She rounded the corner, looked beyond the doors, and screamed.

Darrin lay on the gurney with bandages wrapped around his head and gauze pads covering his eyes. Streaks of blood still ran down his cheeks and stained his collar.

"Oh my God, Darrin!" Olivia cried out.

"Are you his mother?" the paramedic asked.

"Yes, yes I am," she said, stroking her son's hair. "What happened?"

"He has lost the use of his eyes and...."

"My son was blind," she mumbled.

"Mommy? I could see; Daddy helped me see again," Darrin whispered.

"What happened, baby?"

"I could see, but I saw something else too, and it did this. I stopped it, I stopped it, Mommy. I saved everyone in the building except Daddy, Uncle Edward, and Mr. Tony."

Olivia wiped a tear from her eye and looked up to the paramedics. "Can I come in?"

"Yeah, you can ride with him to the hospital. We have the bleeding stopped and he's alert."

Quickly, wanting to be close to her son, she climbed aboard and sat next to Darrin. Think white gauze and wraps covered his face and obscured his cherubic features. Dark red fluid seeped from the bandages, and her heart went out to her son.

"Can I see it? Can I see what happened to my son's eyes?" Olivia sobbed.

One of the paramedics leaned close to her and whispered, "Your son has been through a great ordeal. We have the wound dressed and sterilized, so I wouldn't advise touching it."

"But I have to know!"

The paramedic reached for her and missed her as she rushed to her son's side in the ambulance's cramped space.

Olivia placed her fingers underneath the bandage and lifted. She stifled back a scream when she saw her son's eyes were scratched out and his eyeballs were reduced to bloody chunks in his eye sockets. Blood tears still trailed down his cheeks.

"I had to close the gate; I put the Sleeper back in the void and the voices stopped."

Olivia hugged her son harder and wept while the search for her husband went on, and dawn approached from the east.

Maternal Instinct

O. D. Hegre

"Don't that hurt, Mrs. B?"

Mary Billingham didn't mind—actually kind of liked the nickname. She had no idea the island boys called her that because of her ample breasts. Toby had only recently become aware of the fact and he was now staring at one of those boobs. Even before the latest baby, Mrs. B had no trouble filling out a pair of double-D cups.

"It does hurt, some." Mary moved the newborn to her other arm.

Toby could see one of the baby's cheeks was already turning a kind of greenish-brown.

"Could you get that bottle of pills from the counter over there," Mary raised her arm, pointing over her shoulder, "and a glass of water, please. Thank you, Toby. Oh … and grab yourself something from the fridge, if you like."

Toby sat back down at the kitchen table as Mrs. B finished washing down the pills. *Oxy*-something, it said on the bottle. He'd heard the big kids talking about stuff like that. 'Good shit,' they had said.

"Baby Jill here just got a little frisky this morning." Mary Billingham looked down and made a feeble effort to cover herself. "That's all."

That's all! Toby thought. Christ, he could see that half the nipple on her right breast was gone, replaced by a bulging mass of yellow goop that oozed some white stuff along with an occasional dribble of blood.

"The pills help—some." Mary again sipped the water, rocking the baby gently. "You don't look so good yourself, Toby."

Toby pushed at his right eye until he felt it slip back into the socket. And when it did, his left index finger fell onto the table. "Ahhh, I'm okay I guess." Toby took a slug of the milk; half the mouthful gurgled out of the festering hole in his cheek and ran down his neck. What got past his remaining taste buds tasted like shit. "How'd this happen, Mrs. B? How'd this happen?"

"I'm really not sure. 'Course we all know it was the fish, but the rest of it…."

"I figured you'd have some idea, being a doctor and all."

"I'm a P.A.—a physician's assistant, son."

"Well that's something, ain't it?" Toby stared at the finger, then gently pushed it off the edge of the table.

Mary again rocked the baby. "I figure it's gotta have something to do with hormones. We all ate the fish—everyone on the island ate the fish, but none of the women died. Everyone else—the men, the boys, the girls—everyone else…."

Toby watched as Mrs. B drifted somewhere, her eyes staring out at something he couldn't see.

"Maybe the fish were related to those puffers the Japanese like so much. They *were* delicious." Mary shook her head. "The men had never seen 'um around here before and there were so many." Mary popped another pink pill. "Everyone thought the economy of the island would boom again with the renewal of the fishing. Wouldn't have to depend on those damn cruise ships with those 'blankity-blank' foreigners traipsing all over the island every few weeks." Mary sipped her water. "Tetrodotoxin or something like that, maybe. It's a neurotoxin, paralyzes the muscles. Sometimes, with a small amount of the poison, you think the person is dead, but then it wears off and they come back to life. "

"Zombies? Like in Haiti, Mrs. B?" Toby smiled.

"Yes. Like zombies except—" Mary again sipped her water. "The children really loved those fish, those deadly fish. They ate a lot of them and they died like all the rest. No doubt about it. They died. Every last one of them." Mary looked up at Toby.

"But on the island, only the dead children came … came back to life."

"Yes Toby, only the kids."

"How come only the kids, Mrs. B? How come?"

"Like I said, Toby, hormones. Maybe hormones."

"Huh?"

Mary had thought about it a lot: Adult levels of estrogen may have protected the women from the poison in the first place, and it may have been the low levels of growth hormone that allowed the pre-adolescents to 'recover'—to come back. But God, when they came back … when they came back they—

"I don't get it."

"It's complicated, Toby. Complicated."

"Mrs. B, I just don't get it."

"Ouch!" Mrs. B squirmed in her seat. "Darn. So that's where they are. Ouch!" Mrs. B bent down.

Toby followed her. Beneath the table, at Mrs. B's feet, were the twins, Jenny and Jenna. The skin on their arms and legs was all bubbly with green pus dripping everywhere. They were each chewing on something that hung between their red lips. Toby could see blood dripping from the jagged wounds on Mrs. B's ankles, where the two five-year olds had each ripped off a chunk of skin down to the gleaming white bone. There were other wounds on both of Mrs. B's legs, up as far as Toby dared look.

Mrs. B had straightened back up. She popped another pinky and continued to wince occasionally as she again drifted off to someplace Toby couldn't follow.

Toby swirled the milk in his glass. He'd found his own place to wander, and his thoughts were making him very anxious. It had been three weeks and now it seemed like… seemed like only the moms were left. "What happens, Mrs. B, when—"

Mrs. B had returned from her reverie, looking him straight in the eye. "I checked the schedule down at the wharf yesterday. Three days and the Carnival Line's *Splendor* docks. There will be plenty then, Toby. Don't you worry."

Mrs. B took out two more of the pink pills, popped them in her mouth, and finished her water. "Now. You wanna stay for lunch, Toby?" A smile appeared on Mrs. B's face—a sad smile, but a smile.

"Awe…" Toby found himself staring at that huge mass beneath Mrs. B's blouse. "Nah … I'd better get on home and—"

"Now you listen, young man. A mother's gotta do what a mother's gotta do for her kids. You know that, Toby." With her free hand, Mary pulled up her blouse. "Your momma is doing her best, I am sure of that. But with all your brothers and sisters? I can see you're hungry, boy. You've been looking at this all morning. Don't be shy. You get yourself on over here."

Toby was smiling now too and he slid his chair on across, over to Mary Billingham's side of the table.

As Toby laid his head against her bare breast, Mary ran her fingers through his matted hair, avoiding the open area where brain tissue glistened in the dim light. She'd always wanted a son. Then Mary winced in pain again. "Now Toby, you leave some for the baby, ya hear." Toby nodded his head against the warm flesh, then took a second bite.

Red Leaves

Marc Sorondo

Art itself was a mystery to Julian. This piece in particular was especially enigmatic.

Julian's obsession with art was fueled by his inability to create it. He'd tried many times, spent desperate years trying to fulfill the creative urge, to bring something powerful and beautiful into the world. His mind could envision things, but his body lacked the gift required to give his ideas form. He'd painted and sculpted, dabbled in carving and drawing, but his hands distorted his vision.

His many failures had broken that part of him that hoped his genius remained hidden, waiting for him to stumble onto the proper medium. Now, hopeless, he replaced the need to create with one to collect. He'd spent years and millions of dollars; he'd cashed in favors and made enemies, and it had all been worth it. Julian possessed one of the most impressive private collections in the world.

His newest acquisition was, in Julian's opinion, the crowning jewel of the entire collection. It was beautiful and ominous, and it was an artifact that perfectly represented the mystery that was art.

It was titled *Red Leaves*, though there was not a single leaf in the entire piece. Painted nearly one hundred years ago, it was not done in any style common at that time. It was realistic, so much so that it could be confused for a blown up photograph from even a short distance away.

Red Leaves was painted almost entirely in shades of grey. It depicted a medieval Italian piazza, all dirty cobblestones below and sooty bricks behind. The square was empty aside from a central fountain, one lorded over by a stone angel frozen at its center. The angel's wings were spread behind her; her hands reached forward, as if to embrace the painting's observer.

It was so simple … and yet it wasn't. It had that quality that separated real art from everything else, the indescribable essence that only a gifted hand could capture. The face of the angel, serene, regal, perfect, drew the eye. It alone was enough to classify the painting as the work of a master.

And then, much to Julian's delight, there was the mystery that had surrounded the piece from the very beginning.

The artist was a man named Calen Scratch. Nothing was known of his biography. No other works had ever turned up that could be attributed to him or tied to him in any way. The painting stood as the only record of Scratch's existence.

The painting's first owner was a man named Edminster who had grown wealthy selling lumber in New England.

He'd owned the painting for just under six months when he disappeared. It happened during a particularly vicious blizzard. One moment his family had left him in his study, sitting beneath the outstretched arms of the painted angel; the next, he was gone, the wind and snow of the storm obscuring any trail he may have left. Edminster was never seen again.

Edminster's widow sold the painting to a man named Blum, who had initially intended to donate it to his alma mater to adorn its great hall. He'd decided, shortly after acquiring it, to keep it for himself. It hung on the wall opposite Blum's desk for three months. It was there, the angel staring out at him, as Blum rigged up a noose over his desk and hung himself. He dangled there, bulging eyes locked on the painting, over a note he'd left on his desk. The note was brief, written in a hurried hand, as if Blum had believed he had very little time in which to kill himself. He no longer wanted to live, he'd explained, because there was so much evil in the world, so much blood ... so much blood. Blum's widow didn't touch that room aside from having the noose removed. She'd left it for him as if he'd come back someday and have more work to do.

Two years later someone robbed Blum's home. Only *Red Leaves* was stolen.

It was lost for a very long time after that. It may have been lost forever, except for the painting's seemingly magnetic attraction for tragedy. It was found in the home of a drug smuggler nearly seventy years after it had been stolen. The smuggler, one Antonio Vega, was presumed dead. All that was found of him was a puddle of blood and a series of bullet holes in the walls. The authorities chalked the killing up to a rival drug lord and spent little time actually searching for the body or the killer. Whatever had actually happened to Vega, that painting had seen it all, hung on the wall over the puddle of scarlet that was left behind.

The next owner was a man named Ronald Casey, a real estate mogul who'd purchased the painting as an investment and kept it hidden away in a climate-controlled warehouse, unappreciated like a coin in a piggy bank. Julian had begged Casey to sell the painting, offered outlandish amounts for it, but Casey always refused.

Julian smiled. Casey was dead, killed by a massive heart attack less than a month ago, and his money hungry kids had already sold that painting to Julian. He knew they were selling other precious pieces as well, bloating the dollar amount of their inheritances so they could buy palatial homes, exotic cars, and generally squander their father's hard work.

Julian's butler, Winston, entered and found his employer just as he'd been when he'd left the room fifteen minutes earlier: arms limp at his sides, mouth opened slightly, eyes wide, standing before his newest acquisition.

"Still admiring it, sir?"

"I don't know that I'll ever stop admiring it, Winston. Isn't it beautiful?" Julian said without taking his eyes from it.

Winston looked at the painting. He found it drab, oppressively so. The statue at its center made him think of an adornment on an ornate tombstone. There was no life to the picture. Quite the opposite, Winston thought the painting was dead, soulless.

"I've a crude eye, sir. I'm not one to appreciate the finer points of a work of art." Winston waited a moment. "Sir, I hate to interrupt, but the museum gala begins in less than an hour."

Julian nodded. He took one last look at the angel's face and then turned away.

*　*　*

Julian had studied *Red Leaves* for a bit every day for nearly two months. Some days, when especially busy, he'd spend a very few minutes looking it over. Other days he'd become lost in it, walking in that piazza, viewing the fountain from different angles, only to discover that he'd spent hours standing before the painting.

He knew that piece, knew every bit of it so well he could close his eyes and recreate it exactly on the canvas of his mind. He knew that painting as if it were a part of him, so, when he noticed the single leaf blown against the bottom of the fountain by some Italian breeze not previously alluded to in the painting, Julian gasped.

He leaned in, examining it from inches away. It was crimson, like a spattered droplet of blood on the canvas. When he looked closely, however, Julian could see Scratch's photorealistic detail, the veining of the dead leaf, the way its dried edges curled.

It was, Julian realized with a sense of horror, something that belonged, something that must have always been there. He had somehow overlooked that striking, brilliant detail. He'd somehow been lost in those shades of grey, fallen so deep into them, that he couldn't even see that small splash of color.

Julian felt as if he'd been lying to himself, hiding something away from his own awareness. He stared at the painting, studied it, determined to know its every secret.

* * *

Julian summoned Winston to the gallery with the push of a button and a buzz sent through an intercom. He waited, standing before *Red Leaves*, a sheen of sweat on his forehead, a slight tremor in the hand that he'd brought to his mouth.

"Sir?" Winston said as he entered.

Julian waved him over without saying a word.

"Yes?" Winston said as he stopped beside his employer.

"Tell me, Winston," Julian said. He pointed to the base of the fountain. "What do you see?"

Winston looked at Julian and found him to be serious; more so, he found that Julian almost looked afraid. "Well, I see … leaves. Three red leaves."

"Exactly," Julian said. "Do you recall having seen those leaves before?"

Winston thought of his initial impression of the painting and recalled only that he'd thought there was so much grey. "I can't say I remember them, sir … but … isn't the painting called *Red Leaves*?"

"It is, Winston. It is." Julian leaned forward so that the tip of his nose nearly touched the canvas. "And I had never understood why before…," he whispered.

"Sir?" Winston said. "Can I do something for you?"

Julian shook his head as if rousing himself from a daze. "Yes, I'm sorry. I was a bit distracted. Would you make me an espresso, please? I'm feeling a bit drowsy."

Winston nodded. "Of course. Shall I bring it here or…."

"I'll have it in the library. I'll be heading there in just a minute."

Winston nodded again. Then he turned and left.

Julian looked at the painting. Either it was changing or he was. He couldn't tell which of those possibilities was more terrible. He thought that art itself was a mystery, but that this piece was so shrouded in the unknown and the unknowable, it was obscured by so many layers of uncertainty, it was like a question without an answer, a puzzle with no solution. Art was a wonder, doubly so because no one could really understand how it came into being. This painting though … Julian wanted to understand it, but he wasn't sure that was possible.

* * *

Winston came into the gallery and, as expected, found Julian standing before that damned painting again. He feared that Julian was slipping into some madness, that his obsession with the painting was consuming him.

"Ah, Winston," Julian said with a smile that his butler didn't recognize. He waved Winston over to stand beside him. "You recall that I summoned you a few weeks ago and asked you to look at three leaves blown against the fountain in his painting?"

"I do." Winston wanted to grab Julian by the collar, to shake him and shout at him to sell the damned painting and never think of it again.

"Good. Tell me, when you looked upon the painting last, did you note these?" He motioned to a pair of leaves, frozen in time as they skittered over the cobblestones near the edge of the frame.

Winston looked from the two scarlet leaves to Julian's face. He thought, with a mixture of terror and pity, that Julian had begun drawing leaves in, taking time and care to make sure that they were perfect, that they blended in with the artist's style exactly. He thought that Julian's crushed dreams of artistic greatness were manifesting themselves in these subtle vandalizations. "I don't remember seeing them last time, sir, though I was focused only on those three."

"Indeed, as I had thought myself at first." Julian was quiet for a moment. "Please take a good look at it now, Winston. Take in its every detail. Be careful to note the number and positioning of the crimson leaves."

Winston nodded and looked at the painting. He tried to see where Julian's work differed from that of Calen Scratch. Instead he found that Julian's hand had mimicked the style of the painting perfectly. Winston wondered at the connection between genius and madness.

After a few moments, Winston looked at Julian and said, "I believe I've noted them, sir."

Julian considered this. "Thank you. That will be all."

* * *

Winston cringed as he entered the gallery. "You rang for me, sir?"

"Yes. I was hoping you'd take a look at something for me." Julian motioned to the painting.

Winston gasped. "Sir, I don't understand."

"And how could you … how could anyone hope to understand?" Julian said.

The leaves were everywhere now. A pile had formed at the base of the fountain. Others were blown against the stone angel, pressed against her feet, curled around the fingers of her outstretched hand and held there by the breeze. Leaves numbering in the hundreds were scattered about the cobblestone of the piazza. Every leaf was the same shade of crimson, each one like a spot of blood flicked from the end of a saturated brush.

"It's terrible," Winston muttered.

"Yet somehow beautiful," Julian said.

They were quiet for a moment, both looking at the painting.

Then Winston said, "Sir, forgive me for asking, but … did you do this?"

Julian smiled. "You flatter me to suggest that I could make such masterful additions. I could not paint with such skill."

"Are you certain? Can you be sure?"

Julian's smile fell away. "What are you suggesting, Winston?"

"Sir, I mean no disrespect, but you've been … well, you haven't been yourself since you purchased this piece."

Julian sighed. He looked at the painting. "I can see why you would suspect some sort of insanity. I'm always alone in here. There's no way for you to know what's been going on."

"I'm worried for you," Winston said.

Julian nodded.

"Why not sell this piece, or you could donate it to the museum, or…."

Julian held up his hand, and Winston fell silent. "That is out of the question, Winston."

"I understand, sir, but…."

"That will be all, Winston," Julian interrupted.

Winston nodded. He looked down at his feet, turned, and walked out of the gallery.

Julian watched Winston's back as he walked away. Then he watched the door close. He felt his eyes itching to see the painting; the muscles in his neck almost seemed to twitch in anticipation of turning to face it. He forced his gaze to remain locked on that closed door.

The possibility that this was all some sort of madness, that he was adding those leaves, had never dawned on him. He sought within himself and found that he couldn't be sure, not really. How could he trust his memories when they defied reality? He wasn't sure if it was harder to accept that he was crazy or that an old painting was changing by itself.

Then a flash of motion caught the corner of Julian's eye. He turned and found a single red leaf moving across the canvas of the painting in jerky tumbles as if driven by an inconstant wind. He almost thought he could hear the faint scratching of the leaf's progress over the cobblestone.

Julian wasn't sure if he could trust his own eyes. He wondered, if he knew enough to question the reality of what he saw, did that mean he could trust his senses?

He looked down at his hands. They were trembling. He brought them to his face, covered his eyes, and said, "No more."

When he pulled his hands away, he found that the painting was a chaos of movement. Leaves shifted in the breeze, collecting into piles at the base of the fountain and the four corners of the piazza, swirling in the air currents in the open spaces.

Julian could hear it now, the wind passing through the

narrow alleys between ancient buildings and forcing dry leaves to dance on the stone ground. He even found that he could smell it, that the air inside the gallery was crisp and cool and held the scent of turned foliage.

Julian shook his head as if denying the painting, as if he refused to accept what he saw, but he trusted; deep down he knew that his eyes did not lie to him. He knew that the mystery of *Red Leaves* went far beyond a few coincidental misfortunes and an obscure artist. This mystery went so much deeper than all that.

It terrified Julian, but he was also drawn to it. If his other pieces were art, what was *Red Leaves*? If masters had painted the other works that adorned the walls of his gallery, who or what had painted this scene? As if in answer to both those questions and a million others that he'd yet to think of, Julian's mind whispered, *Something more.*

He could feel the breeze now, cooling his face and tousling his hair. He looked down and found that he was ankle deep in a sea of scarlet leaves that shifted with the wind.

Julian could no longer tell where the painted world stopped and the real world began. He could no longer be sure there was any difference between the two.

He looked up at the face of the angel and exhaled all the air from his lungs in a rush when he saw her stone eyes looking back at him. Her outstretched hands seemed to be reaching out to embrace him. Her spread wings seemed ready to enfold him.

Julian inhaled and held the breath. It was so beautiful. He wanted to touch her, to feel her hands on his face and the downy grey softness of her wings wrapped around his body.

She reached for Julian and he stepped toward her. His

hand touched her cheek; it was hard and cold. Her hands touched him and they were like the hands of death: cold, lifeless, unforgiving.

The angel's stone hands wrapped around Julian's throat.

He grabbed them, tried to pry them from his neck. In his struggle, he looked up at her serene face, into her unblinking eyes. She was horrible and beautiful. She was everything he loved and feared at once. She was truly a work of art.

He studied her face even as black spots formed in his vision and popped like bubbles. Even when his sight blurred and faded to black, he saw her face in his mind.

* * *

Winston knocked at the door, not wanting to barge in unannounced. "Sir?" he called when Julian did not answer.

He waited another moment. "Sir?" he called again.

Finally, he pushed the door open. The gallery was empty but the light was still on. He walked in, thinking he would turn it off before going to find Julian.

He reached the light switch and reached out but paused when his fingers touched it. He looked in the direction of the painting; he couldn't see it from that angle.

He'd never had the chance to examine it without Julian present. He didn't want to waste the opportunity to look at those leaves without anyone watching.

He walked over, part of him dreading the sight of all that crimson on the canvas.

Then he saw it was all stone in shades of grey. There was not a single leaf remaining. Winston wasn't sure how such a thing could be done, but he knew very little about art. He leaned in and sought some sign of the paint that had been added, but he found nothing.

A chill ran up Winston's spine.

He turned and rushed toward the light. He was pleased to leave the painting in darkness where no one could see it. For reasons he couldn't understand, it felt safer that way.

THE ROSY BOA

SEAN MORELAND

When Cyan finally asked me if I wanted to stay over at his house that weekend, I was thrilled to the point of nausea, as if everything in my stomach had suddenly transubstantiated into some too-fizzy soft drink. I'd been crazy for Cyan for nearly a year, although I still didn't really understand what that meant. I know, that must sound naive to you. You're young, yes, but surely more worldly than I was then. But that was another place, another time.

Cyan was the first great love of my life. I'd had that passing glimmer of attraction, that feeling that goes beyond the basic affinity of friendship, for a *few* boys by that point. But while I thought about those transient feelings often, especially late at night, lying awake in my darkened room, I never said anything about them to anyone. And *since* they were transient, I think I hoped they might just pass away entirely, and I could get on with having what I then thought of as a *normal* life.

Of course, those feelings never did go away, not exactly. But after what happened with Cyan, they *changed*, fundamentally.

I didn't know if Cyan was ... well, if Cyan felt the way that I felt. We'd become fairly good friends, but I was always a little on guard, precisely because I felt so strongly for him, was so attracted to him. We'd only hung out outside of school a few times, and we'd never been intimate, physically, aside from, you know, a couple of friendly scraps, grapples that linger a little, your hands both too-conscious of the fine skin and young muscle against them. Once or twice, when we were alone in the park, he'd clasped me, suddenly, close to him, so that our cheeks touched. That was as close as we'd gotten, but I thought, *those moments must've meant to him what they meant to me, right?*

But still, I didn't really know. Nobody used the word *gaydar* back in those days, but even if they *had, I* didn't seem to have it. And of course, *of course*, we never *talked* about the way we felt about one another. No, no way. That would have been, as we would've said back then, *totally gay*! Awful phrase, isn't it? Well, it was the eighties, and I lived in a small town. What could you do?

There was only one kid in our high school that openly admitted to being gay, and he got ragged pretty regularly for it. That was one reason for my never talking about the way that I felt. That, and of course my charming father. He'd told me once, when I was ten, that if *some fag* ever hit on him, he'd *bust his face up bad*, and that if either I or my brother turned out to be a *fag*, he would have to disown us, kick us out on the street. You'll find this hard to believe, since you obviously come from a good home, a *loving* family, but he meant it, my dad. He would've. He eventually kicked my brother out for smoking pot, of all things, but that's another story.

Whatever else you might say about my dad, he was a forthright bastard. You knew *right* where things stood with him. So I figured if I *was* a *fag*, and I wasn't even *sure* I was, I'd better keep it to myself, at least until I was out of that idiotic high school, and away from my father's itchy fists, his tyrannical intolerance.

I wasn't sure what I was, but I knew beyond a shadow of a doubt that what I *felt* for Cyan was powerful, beautiful and true. Hard to explain that certainty, especially if *you've* never felt it before—have you? Well, it doesn't matter, I suppose. Love is a little different for each of us, isn't it? And a little different each time, too. Like me and you, like *this*, this unique togetherness.

What was it about Cyan that called all my blood to attention, caused my stomach to take flight, my heart to flutter? It wasn't any one thing, of course, but *everything* about him. Beginning with his name—I'd heard it called in class, in the ninth grade, before I'd ever seen his face.

Kee-ahn. I was surprised when I saw how it was spelled months later, seeking out his image in the yearbook. Written like that shade of green-and-blue, but sounded differently, like the cry of some exotic bird.

Oh, Cyan *was* beautiful. Thin, taut, toned, smooth-skinned, his hair rising from his lovely face like the plume of that exotic bird whose cry gave him his name, Miss Clairol black with a feathered streak of red at the left temple. He glammed better than anybody else I knew, and bravely. None of the knuckle-draggers we were caged with could quell his fierce beauty.

But it wasn't just his name, and it wasn't just those looks, that style, that lit all the nether fires my teenaged body could barely contain. It was his soul, fearless, but somehow surrendered to the world, embracing it, not fighting vainly against it, like all the other kids seemed to be, like I was, hiding behind my little walls even where he was concerned, keeping my love for him hidden like forbidden letters under the dirty mattress of my heart.

But then came that fateful Friday, when Cyan told me his parents were out of town for the weekend, and asked me if I wanted to come over, maybe watch some movies, keep him company while they were gone. He'd rented some trashy horror flicks from Bandito Video. It was all VHS tapes back then. I don't know if you're old enough to remember that.

I managed to spurt out a *sure* that didn't sound as non-chalant as I wanted it to, but that was at least more intelligible than the desperate yelp I'd been afraid would issue from my mouth. He gave me the address. I already knew it by heart, since I'd looked his father's name up in the phonebook weeks before, but I didn't tell him that.

For the rest of the day, I floated on some cottony cloud with lightning for legs. I daydreamt through my classes, gazed longingly out the window on the bus ride home, was immune to my father's brutishness, my mother's cluelessness, my brother's taunts. The knowledge that I would soon see Cyan again, be alone with him, be able, maybe for the first time, to share my feelings with him, acted like a force-field between me and all that was worst about my world.

It was about seven when I slipped out of the house, muttering something to my folks like *watching movies with some guys from school, we're all gonna crash at my buddy Regie's, his number's on the fridge.* I think I named Regie because I didn't want to taint Cyan's name by pronouncing it in the oppressively mundane presence of my parents.

Whatever exactly I said, it seemed to satisfy them— Dad went right back to his hockey game, and Mom to her knitting, after proclaiming a perfunctory, *Be careful, honey.*

It took me almost half an hour to bike to Cyan's house, which was set up on a hill, surrounded by shady trees, on the outside edge of the suburbs. It was one of the loveliest neighbourhoods in the town, and most of the residents were pretty wealthy. My dad used to joke about the houses there *looking down on* the town below. It always seemed to me, though, that they were looking up at a sky that I imagined being clearer from that elevated vantage.

I slid my bike between a bush and the side of the house, some instinct telling me to make it as inconspicuous as possible, and walked with deliberate slowness to the front door, which was closed, golden light radiating out from the arced window just above head height. I noted the brass-inlaid doorbell, but knocked instead. Despite the relative isolation of the place, I felt gazes fixed on me from the neighbouring houses, suspicious slits of their lit windows winking judgmentally at me through the hushing trees.

Cyan answered quickly. He was dipped in tight black jeans and a Siouxsie Sioux tee, his hair as huge and beautiful as I'd ever seen it. He led me into a lush living room, where he was watching MTV. When I confessed that we didn't have cable at home, and so I almost never got to watch music videos, he dug out a tape on which he'd recorded a slew of videos. Depeche Mode, Siouxsie, the Cure, Echo and the Bunnymen, that kind of thing. Sitting there, so close to him, seeing videos to songs I'd never known I loved so much, I was in some mad mix of heaven and hell.

Feeling tiny beside him, in the shadow of his architectural hair, awkwardly bolted to that giant sofa, I felt like I was made of icing-sugar. If his hand or leg brushed me, even for an instant, I was afraid I'd either melt, or shatter into a million shards, and I was afraid he could hear how crazy-fast my heart was beating.

Every time I got near to working up the nerve to say something to him, he would say, *hey, check this out*, and cue up another video. Finally, he'd either played, or fast-forwarded through, every video on the tape, and after a few seconds of static, he clicked STOP on the remote. The tape stopped, and up popped the local evening news. I remember the blonde-helmeted talking head clearly, but little of the news that spouted from her rubbery pink mouth, something about cutbacks, the closure of hospitals, patients turned out on the streets. I was too on fire with Cyan's nearness, and he was too eager to liberate a couple of his father's beers from the fridge, to pay any attention.

After we cracked the beers, drank a few slugs, I began to hope that the warm lubricity unleashed in me would make me better able to open up to Cyan. It was a brief eternity and three bottles later, though, that, heart in mouth, I breathed deeply and prepared to broach the too-tender subject of my too-intense feelings. Before I could, Cyan asked, out of the blue, if I wanted to go upstairs and see his mother's *rosy boa*.

I'd seen rosy boas in the Toronto zoo, and my first reaction was incredulity that Cyan's mother, who was a straight, chronically power-suited, sternly lined lawyer with an all-business nut-brown bob cut, would have a pet boa. I could easily picture Cyan with a big snake wrapped around his neck, draping down his chest. But then, I could easily picture Cyan in all kinds of contexts, clothed or otherwise. But that his *mother* would keep one as a pet just didn't sit right.

Suddenly, my mouth hanging open in the prelude to a reply, I forgot about the oddity of the snake as my attention slid back to Cyan's asking me if I wanted to go *upstairs*!

I forced out the same stupid *sure* that I'd managed earlier at school, and followed Cyan as he thumped enthusiastically up the great polished-wood staircase to the second floor. I felt like a total idiot when he ushered me into his parents' grandiose bedroom, and made for a tall, antique-looking wood wardrobe. He opened the mirrored door, and drew out a delicate accessory, passed down from a better-dressed era than our own.

The boa was beautiful, hugely, magnificently feathered, its colour tipping from a dusky rose to a coral to a pale, pale pink at the base of each feather, and it rippled and shimmered as Cyan threw it, gleefully, around his neck, did a high-kicking, fetchingly hilarious parody of a burlesque dancer. It moved with him, made his otherwise jerkily exaggerated gestures seem balletic, but also vaguely alien.

I clapped my hands and laughed, the laughter made almost painful by the perplexed arousal that drove it up out of my body. Then, Cyan threw that beautiful boa around my neck, and I danced, too, feeling freer than I'd ever felt before.

During that whole mad dance, I felt like a kiss was imminent. Each gesture seemed to move us closer to a point of precious contact that I craved … but that never seemed to come.

Finally, after what might've been an hour of spinning, capering, bopping, and bowing, we fell together in an exhausted heap on the floor, his face close to mine, his breath hot and fast on my cheek.

I moved my head ever-so-slightly, and my lips brushed his … and suddenly the room crashed down into darkness. I gave a small cry of startled frustration, and Cyan sat up abruptly.

"Did a fuse blow?" I asked him.

"I don't know," he said. As one, we crept to the window, looked out on the tree-lined neighbourhood. Here, the houses were much further apart than in the little suburb I so grudgingly called home, but even so, we'd been able to see the lights from three of the nearer houses before. Now, there was nothing; just the vague, swaying suggestions of nearby trees, and a stretching, moonless darkness.

"Looks like it's out all over town," Cyan observed. I agreed, wishing I felt confident enough to grab his hand and hold it.

"Well, we've got some flashlights down in the basement. Want to go down there with me and find them?"

I said, "Sure," although my legs felt like dried rubber; hard to move, likely to break.

We'd made it out of the bedroom, halfway down the hall toward the stairs that led to the ground floor landing when we first heard it.

The sound rose up from below, shattering nerves and freezing limbs. It was an arrhythmic, percussive pulse, *whump ... whump .... whump.*

In that dark hallway, I fumbled for Cyan, my hands clambering at his arms, shoulders, neck, my right hand folding over the boa which now hung limply, forgotten, around his neck. A cold fist clamped my heart. I felt his hand fold over mine, folded over that boa, its fine pink feathers crushed in our panicked grips. Clutching his hand, I whispered, "O god what is that?"

As one in our shared terror, we rushed back into his parents' bedroom and slammed the door closed behind us. We leaned heavily against it, our sides pressed together, to keep out whatever force menaced us from the noisy darkness without.

We remained there, rigid, until the sound suddenly ceased. The house fell silent; the room felt full of our rapidly syncopated breaths, all-too audible now in the absence of that other horrible noise.

Cyan spoke first, a forced-sounding half-laugh in his voice.

"I think we've just scared ourselves stupid."

"I guess so," I agreed, although my voice quavered audibly. It was like Cyan derived new confidence from my persistent fear, for he laughed low again, more believably this time.

"There's a bat," Cyan said, "my dad keeps it under the bed. I'm going to get it."

"OK," I replied. His warmth moved away through the dark, his sneakers scuffing quietly across the floor, and I heard him fumbling for something. Then he was back, his hand on my shoulder, reassuringly. Then, in an act I found indescribably touching, he folded the boa around my neck, wrapped it twice like it was a scarf he was using to warm me, as though my shivering came not from fear, but simple cold. I fell against and clung to him in that dark room in that huge, dark house, with that moonless night outside. Still, un-banished by Cyan's heat, a cold dread crept up and down my spine, its dance unlike the joyous one that Cyan, the boa, and I had done earlier.

We held one another for some immeasurable passage in time, and the fear finally began to drain from my body, replaced by the warmth that glowed invisibly from his.

Then the sound came again, louder, faster, seemingly closer this time, and I choked down the scream that tried to explode from my throat.

Whumpwhump WHUMP, came that terrible clamour.

I clung to Cyan, and he to me, and we were closer in our shared terror than I'd ever been with anyone before. Cyan's breath came faster in my face and my body trembled helplessly against his.

Suddenly, the rhythm of Cyan's breath changed, and his gasps of terror turned to relieved laughter, unforced this time.

"The window!" he declared. "The basement window! My dad opened it before they left this morning to air out the dampness down there! It's just the window, clattering in the wind!"

He let out a loud laugh of genuine relief that, somehow, still didn't penetrate my paralyzing dread. "Come on," he insisted, "we're being totally ridiculous! It's just this crazy wind! Let's go down, close it, and get some flashlights, or maybe some candles."

"Sure," I croaked, trying to force myself to believe him. He pulled away, and I heard a click as he turned the doorknob, prepared to face the corridor, the stairs, and whatever lay beyond.

My hand reached out of its own will and seized his shoulder and I hissed, "Don't go," in a voice that sounded so pleading I felt sick at myself. "I don't think it's the window," I warned him. I had, and still have, no idea why I was so sure that something more dangerous was at the root of that sound, but the feeling was unshakeable.

Cyan laughed again and shook his head. He said, and these were his exact words, I swear: "Don't *be* such a *fag*." He had shrugged off my hand and was halfway out the door by now. I was shocked and angry at hearing that word, so beloved of my meathead father, coming from Cyan's lovely beak. I think the anger helped to quell the wheedling note of fear in my voice as I said, "At least take the bat, OK? Just in case?" I think he nodded, and he moved back into the room and bent down.

That percussive sound ceased again, as suddenly as it had begun. Then I heard a metallic *thunk* as the bat knocked the bedpost, and Cyan moving back toward the still-open door.

"It's stopped," I said lamely.

"It's just going to start again when the wind picks up if I don't go down and close it. Besides, we need those flashlights. Why don't you just come with me? You're being ridiculous."

All I could say was, "I know. But I can't." And I couldn't. I swear, I tried, but I couldn't make my body move past that threshold. I couldn't convince myself that there wasn't something awful waiting down there. Instead, and without knowing why, I unravelled the boa from my neck and shoulders, and fumblingly wrapped it around his as he brushed past me.

"For luck," I whispered, ashamed at my own cowardice, sure I should be going with him, but unable to make my frozen body obey. Then he was through the door, down the hall, and gone, his sneakers making faint scuffing creaks on the stairs.

I clicked the door closed and leaned against it, breathing rapidly, praying for my irrational fear to dissipate, for Cyan to return and prove me wrong. I wondered where he was – the landing, still? On the next flight of stairs? Or lower, down there in the basement? Had he found the window?

Just as I'd started to hope that he'd been right all along, that he'd found the window, closed it, and was now on his way back to me, that sound started up again, and again it was louder, closer. It was not, I was sure, coming from the basement now, but from the ground floor ... maybe even the landing ... that awful hammering, coming ever closer to the stairs.

Unable to breathe, I stepped backwards into the dark room, fell back as my legs bumped against the bed, and if I'd been able to breathe I'm sure I would have shrieked. As it was, I just slumped back onto the mattress ... but then the sound was gone again, as quickly as it had come.

My breath came back, and I sat there, alone in the dark, panting, panic mingled with fitful hope. And I heard a slow, steady series of scuffing creaks, the sound of footsteps on the stairs.

They were Cyan's footsteps, I was *sure* of it ... but somehow, I was also nightmarishly sure they *weren't*.

They shuffled across the carpeted hallway, and I sat on the bed. My trembling had stopped, my body was perfectly still, perfectly tensed, a rabbit under wolf's eyes.

I heard the quiet rattle of the doorknob, and the slight creak of the door sliding open, and I stayed frozen. I forced myself to squeak, "Cyan?" It was the sound of a starving baby bird.

The footsteps shuffled closer, and I drew my legs up and backed myself across the mattress. It must be Cyan. *He must be* trying *to terrify me, to get back at me for chickening out!*

The footsteps shuffled closer, and I outstretched my arms, across the infinite darkness, toward them ... and my breath exploded from my body in a gasp of relief as my fingers closed around that beautiful rosy boa, and I cried, "Cyan! Thank God! You scared the shit out of me!"

But Cyan said nothing, just stood there in the unbroken dark, his breath, I now noticed, rasping too loudly, as though he were badly congested. I now noticed, too, that the feathers between my clenched fingers were tacky, warmly wet.

My hands slid from the boa to Cyan's chest, felt those tight muscles, felt his t-shirt's strange stickiness, too. They slid over his shoulders and up the back of his neck, my relief at his safe return blowing away the threads of my inhibitions. I bent his head toward mine, searching for his lovely, unseen mouth.

As my lips felt the wet heat of his breath, I was overcome with joy, and I kissed that beautiful mouth, my tongue finding that wetly welcoming portal into the center of Cyan's being. But then my mouth was full of the taste of metal and salt. I pulled back, shocked at the surge of sticky fluid, and my fingers inched from the back of his neck to his throat and into that strange new slit, where they felt blood, bone ... and what I now realize was Cyan's last breath.

As he slumped forward into me, dampening my neck, left shoulder, and chest, I was struck irrevocably with an awareness of how open Cyan was to the world, through this new mouth that had grown below the old one.

And before I knew what I was doing, I had bent my head to kiss it again, the sticky second mouth that this strange night, or something that crept through it, had opened in him.

With that kiss, I knew what I was, or at least, what I was not.

I was not a *fag*, after all. Not *gay*. Not *straight*, either. No. My love runs beyond the realm where words like "girl" or "boy" bear any meaning, beyond the world where genitalia matter. I am one who loves you not for the body you were saddled with at birth, but for what that body can become, once it is opened to the world, the way the lovely, the unforgettable Cyan was.

Which brings me, my beautiful, patient, *quiet* little bird, back to you.

Are you ready, at last, for your turn to speak? Shhhh. Not like that, with words like those. Here, my hands are steady, it'll be quick, and then it'll be intimate beyond *anything* you've ever known.

Yes, like that. We'll just leave the tape over your old mouth. You won't need it, now, with this new one, this perfect mouth, with its rosy, feathered edges, fit like the first one never was, to utter words of love to me, from a place beyond all breath.

WHISPER ME GOODNIGHT

BRANDON KETCHUM

"Whisper me goodnight," she purred in his ear, stealing a kiss on his cheek as he stared at her in disbelief. George Anders would never forget her cruelty, stamped with awful detail upon his inner eye. She had spoken their secret, most tender phrase, but out of spite instead of love. Leila Lavine informed George during her brief visit that she was casting him aside. A new man had captured her heart, she jeered. They were moving into a room at the Public Hotel and Tavern that very night. George had been nothing but a plaything. Her lips twisted into a mock smile as he took in the news. Leila half opened the door to leave, before turning back with feline grace for her disdainful kiss.

As for the rest of the night, George could remember little, but what he did remember was quite clear. The sound of carriages trundling over cobblestones called out in the dark Ambridge night, but it could not overcome the noise of a cat howling in agony. The smog from the smokestacks was thick in the air, enough almost to suffocate one's sense of smell. Through the still-open door, he noticed the lightning bugs flash off and on. Other than that, and for the intervening several days, he could remember nothing.

George snapped back to himself, to the present time, and to his pain. He wanted no visitors; misery and dejection were his boon companions, and he needed nothing but water, a corner of bread, and his own dark thoughts to keep him company.

"Now now, lover," Leila said from the corner. "Don't be so hard on yourself."

George whipped around, shocked almost to death at the sound of her voice. There, in the corner of his dusty room, sitting on a rickety chair, looking like the cat that got the cream, was Leila. His Leila Lavine.

"What? How did you get in, Leila?"

"Why, you brought me here, didn't you, George?" she asked in reply, the ghost of a smile tugging at the corners of her mouth. "Why else would I be here?"

"But I...," George faltered. "But you left me."

"Yet here I am, George."

"Why?"

She laughed aloud, staring straight into his eyes. "George, I'm here to tell you how pathetic you are, how absolutely wretched your life is."

"Damn it, Leila, you stop it."

"Why, George? Truth hurt?"

"It's not the truth," he raged. "I was good to you. I'm a

good man. I loved you more than you deserved, and you damned well know it."

Leila had no response for him but to laugh, and laugh, and laugh some more. She had no need of words, for her peals of laughter annoyed him more than words ever could. He shouted at her to stop, screamed and howled at her. She just laughed on. He began slapping her, first on one cheek, and then the next, repeating several times, but she wouldn't stop laughing. Her cheeks certainly didn't have such a perfect glow about them anymore, but still she laughed.

Finally, George admitted defeat, slinking back across the room to stand with his back to the wall. As Leila continued to laugh, he slid slowly to the floor, drew his knees up to his chest, and hung his head between his legs, giving in to despair. This, finally, seemed to sate her, because Leila stopped laughing.

"What's the matter, George? Cat got your tongue?"

"Just leave me alone," he wailed. George started to cry, the tears flowing easily, and drawing furrows of cleanliness through his dirty face. He hadn't bathed since the night she left him. On and on he sobbed, snot bursting from his nose to run down onto his chest and legs.

"Why George, is something wrong?"

"Why must you torment me?" he asked, his voice hoarse from weeping. "You've taken everything from me already. What more do you want?"

"Well, not *everything*, George, surely. You have a little more to give, don't you?"

"What? I've spent all my money on you, Leila. I have this room, but not for much longer. I don't even own the furniture. What else is there?"

"Your life, silly," she told him, grinning broadly.

"M-my life?" he stammered. "Why would you want my life?"

"You know."

And he did. George didn't want to admit it, especially to himself, but he knew.

"What do you need your life for anymore?" she demanded. Leila's eyes smoldered from across the room, piercing his and seeming to look inside him. "You just told me you haven't anything left. What good is a life without hope?"

"No," he whimpered. "Please don't make me."

"Make you?" she asked with feigned surprise. "How could *I* make *you* do anything? I have no power over you anymore, do I? Or do I?"

"Please, please, Leila, please...,"

"No, don't you *dare* beg me for anything, you bastard." All signs of mockery had left her voice. Leila was all steel and vengeance. "Now give me your life, lover. Give it to me. Now."

"Ah God, no," George whined, slowly levering himself to his feet, bracing against the wall. He kept blubbering incoherently, his eyes red and puffy, welling with tears.

"Yes, George. Now."

Slowly he shuffled across the floor, unable to even pick his feet up off the sticky slats. He barely inched forward, as if his body was fighting the short journey to the center of the room. He didn't want to reach the spot, knowing he would give her his life too, just as he had given her everything else. But he was powerless to stop. He was spellbound, and knew he was in her debt.

"That's right, George, reach on up there. You can feel it

hanging there, can't you? Right where you'll be in a moment."

George was stunned to realize there was something hanging from the ceiling beam above him, almost as if it had been there all along. He gazed at that rope with rapt attention, his sobs ceased, jaw hanging open. He also noted with stunned attention a noose already tied at the end of the rope, inviting him to slide his head through, snug it around his neck, and fall.

"Not yet, George. You would choke for hours, and you might not die at all. No, your life, and your soul, belongs to me. I won't have you rescued. Come, use my chair."

His step was more sure as George walked away from the rope, and towards the chair holding his dearest, most hated Leila. Gently, with over-exaggerated care, he bent a little, and took her up in his arms. George was rather shocked at how light this woman, with the cruelty of a vicious panther, truly was, but no matter. He took her with ease to his bed and laid her there, unconsciously angling her head to see the dangling rope. Then, with something of a renewed sense of vigor, George strode back across the room, recovered the chair and placed it directly under the rope. It hung far enough above him that he imagined it would be just before his face, were he to stand on the chair.

Suddenly, as if a spell had been broken, George snapped back to himself. He was standing in front of the chair, horrified to see he had prepared his own suicide with such alacrity. He looked over at his bed and saw smug satisfaction writ across Leila's pale face.

"Good, George. You've finally done something right. At least in death, you'll prove you're a man."

He couldn't tell if Leila was mocking him, but he figured

she probably was. He imagined that any man with an ounce of self-respect and integrity would look at him with utter loathing, so he guessed it didn't matter if she was mocking him now. All that mattered was his end.

George looked down to find he was no longer standing on the floor, but rather on the chair. When he tried to look back over to the bed, he found it difficult, because the noose was already encircling his neck, and had been tightened. He managed to get his head around and lock gazes with his former paramour one final time.

"Leila," he mewled.

"Whisper me goodnight," she purred.

George fell. As he kicked and bucked in his death throes, George's eyesight began to first blur and lose focus, then fade to black. With the last observation of his dying senses, he could hear a loud clamor at the door. Then his hearing failed him too, and with the mercy of finality, George died.

The newly-formed Ambridge police were calling to investigate, because George Anders' room was beginning to exude a most rotten stench. They burst through the door to find Anders hanging by the neck in the middle of the room, his clothes soiled from tears, snot, and the just-released contents of his bowels. Beneath him lay an overturned chair, clearly used in aiding his suicide. Blood was spattered across the floor, mixing with the dust to form dark splotches of dried paste. Under his bed was the decaying corpse of a young woman, whom they soon surmised to be the missing Leila Lavine, and a saw flecked with flaking, dried blood. Not far from his dangling feet, laying atop his unmade bed, was her decomposed head. The eyelids remained opened, and must have been held that way until rigor mortis had set in.

Ghoulishly enough, Anders must have also taken care to place the head just so, because it was staring at his hanging corpse as it swayed slowly in place.

THE HANGMAN'S KNOT

MASON GALL

The Buick jounced and squeaked its way across Hangman's Road, kicking up clouds of dust into the dry, hot afternoon air. He was already late for work, and there was nothing worse than being late for work when you really didn't want to go. How he hated these dry hangings with their grim sterility and that whip crack of the rope at the end that seemed to carry on into infinity, echoing his own guilt in the act.

The desiccated countryside passed outside his car, the dead and dying trees taunting him with their stillness. There was no breeze at all; this summer was going to be murderously hot. It was already hot, and the townsfolk never acted right when it got like this. The Hangman was going to be very busy this year. Today was only the start.

His attention was captured momentarily by a flash of white outside the driver's side window. Some large, four-legged, skeletal thing was running through the woods parallel to his car, and making little effort by the look of it. The creature was just toying with him, attracted by the thrumming of the Buick's engine. His heart quickened a bit, but only in the way a tourist's heart might quicken on safari when a lion showed up outside the Land Rover. These creatures hadn't shown much interest in attacking cars, and the Hangman was one of the lucky few in town with a working one. It was one of the perks of being the Hangman; they didn't want the one who tied the knot showing up in one of the town wagons with the other rabble-rousers. A drunk Hangman meant a messy Hangman.

The creature, with all of its jutting bones and horns, ran along the edge of the forest for a few more moments, then peeled off and disappeared. He didn't much care for how bold they had become lately, coming out in the daytime like this. In the confines of town the people were safe, or so the Pastor said. *A Holy Pact with God*, Pastor said. *Keep out the Interlopers*, Pastor said. The Hangman didn't know how much of that he believed, but he would never say so out loud. The Pastor did God's work, no doubt, but the Hangman's work was something else entirely.

He turned his gaze up to the rearview mirror and saw nothing but two grizzled, gray eyes staring back at him. Those eyes, colder than they had been years ago, were set in a face that was a roadmap of a hard life, a survival life. The broken blood vessels across his cheeks and nose told of his hard-drinking ways. His mouth turned down in a kind of perpetual scowl. He looked the way a Hangman should.

The job had come to him by accident; he knew how to tie the knot, that was all. He knew to keep the knot cinched under the left side of the jaw, and he had once had working knowledge of math and physics, so he knew how long the rope needed to be to snap the neck cleanly without tearing off the head. He knew how short to make it for a good hang, the one that took a long time for the condemned to die. The math and physics had long since departed his brain, but that didn't matter because the job was all instinct and experience to him now.

Just over the horizon, he could see Gallows Hill approaching. *His* hill. That was something else he had done; he had built the gallows strong and solid. *His* gallows. It had been him from the beginning. And why? Because he could, and because he wanted more for his family. The Hangman got the car and the Hangman's family got to have its own house in town, rather than sharing with two or three others like most families did. The Hangman didn't have to work the fields, bust rocks, or fix the fences with the others, he only had to keep his gallows maintained and ready for its next guest. Except for being the most feared and loathed individual in town, the Hangman was the belle of the ball.

As the forest fell away outside, he heard the crunch of gravel beneath his tires. Gallows Hill rose before him in a large clearing. There were two roads approaching it from town: Gallows Road and this one, Hangman's Road. The Hangman did indeed have his own road. He was more privileged in this life he hated than he ever had been in his old life, the one full of inanity and decency and happiness.

He made a slight left and followed a gentle curve around the base of the hill until he came upon a small outbuilding—really only a bench with a roof over it. Parked next to it was a cherry of an International Harvester pickup, a perfectly maintained 1954 International R110 with a big ugly star painted on the side. It was the Sheriff's truck, and the Hangman had no idea how the man kept it up so well. His own Buick had maybe another five hundred miles or so left on it, and he didn't think the town had enough resources to buy him another one from the scavengers here on the outside.

It was odd to see the truck there, and even odder to see the two men sitting on his bench. He pulled his car to a grinding halt next to the Sheriff's pickup. The men stood as he approached them.

"Yer late, Hangman," the Sheriff said in his tremulous tenor voice, his narrow, shifty weasel eyes darting between him and everything else like they always did.

"Sorry, Sheriff. Had some trouble with the car this morning, probably because of the hot."

"Ain't too good havin' a Hangman who can't—"

The Sheriff's words were halted by the big hand that fell on his shoulder. The Pastor was an enormous man who had been—behind his back, of course—nicknamed Bluto because of his resemblance to the old cartoon bully, thick black beard and all. He had once been an auto mechanic at the local shop, but when things went to hell he had gotten full of the Holy Spirit, or as the Hangman's only friend and drinking buddy, Lane Garrison, said, "Full o' the *Holy Spurt*." How an oversized grease monkey came to be the spiritual leader of a town, the Hangman had no idea.

"Now now, Sheriff," the Pastor said in his slow, deep drawl, "no sense in prodding the man over his tardiness. The town wagon ain't even here, and the condemned is behind them. Let's let the man focus for a few minutes; it's a mighty hard job. Why don't you have a seat, my good son?"

The Pastor, in his dusty denim and black priest's shirt, gestured to the bench, the *Hangman's* bench, the very one he had built with his own two hands. What kind of imperious asshole, self-appointed servant of God or not, invited a man to have a seat on his own bench? And why were they here, anyway? The minutes before a hanging had always been his time of personal reflection, and truthfully, his time to have a few nips from the flask he kept in his pocket. No one sat with him; no one visited. He needed no coaching or motivation. He was the Hangman. This was what he did. He loved his family—his wife, his daughter, his son—but he was solitary by nature. This job was perfect for that; most of the rest of the town left him alone. He had his hood to conceal his identity, but it was more symbolic than anything. Everyone knew him and what he did. He was a man who had once taught mathematics to their teenagers, but now popped the necks of their criminals. The townsfolk didn't exactly dislike him, but they mostly avoided him. The families of the ones he had killed, though, hardly ever spared him a scornful look if he happened to pass them in town. Once, his little girl, Myra, had been spit on by the teenage brother of a young man who had been hanged for stealing. That was the closest his family had ever come to a physical attack, and said expectorator had been handily run out of town, lucky that he himself had not swung from the rope. The Hangman might have enjoyed that one.

The Sheriff removed the stupid straw hat from his narrow head and scratched his red, balding pate. "Well, the wagons are on their way, I can hear 'em. Folks sound well and truly shit-faced from the sound of it."

Sure enough, the Hangman could hear the rumble of the diesel trucks that pulled the wagons. He didn't know how much longer those old beasts would last either; they certainly weren't in the same shape as the Sheriff's truck. The final wagon, the one carrying the condemned, would be pulled by mule. The ride down Gallows Lane from town would be long, bumpy, and brutally hot for the condemned man or woman.

Lord, he thought, *I hope it's not a woman. Maybe that's why they're here.*

He had only done one woman before: Mrs. Mina Barnell, accused by some her fellow townsfolk of witchcraft. The rather pathetic tomatoes she normally grew had sprouted extra red and juicy that year, and instead of accepting the excuse that she had been composting her meager food scraps and using the nutrient rich result in her garden, they accused her of being a witch. She had been arrested, tried, and sentenced by the Sheriff himself—as all the condemned were—and hanged by the Hangman. It had been a messy hang, because the Pastor believed a witch must be beheaded, or the town would risk her returning from the dead and cursing them all. At a mere ninety pounds, Mrs. Barnell had been too light for a messy hang, so the Hangman had had to attach a sack full of rocks to her waist. How her thin flesh had torn at the neck made him sick to think about.

The Hangman never attended the trials, and thus never knew the accused or their crimes until the Sheriff's official pronouncement of guilt just before the switch was pulled. He preferred it that way. Mrs. Mina Barnell, or Ms. Mina as his children called her, had been a neighbor for years, well before the world had gone sour. She had sat at his wife's bedside during her difficult second pregnancy. She had been so damn excited over the tomatoes she had worked so hard to cultivate in this dry and dying land that the Hangman and his family had been the first to taste them, and my, they had been absolutely fine. Juicy and delicious, without a hint of witchcraft or black magic in them.

Mina Barnell, he knew, had never intended to keep a single one of those tomatoes for herself, and yet she had ended her long days on the earth with her head torn off, and her tomatoes likely in a place of honor at the Pastor's privileged table.

"I really think you ought have a seat," the man in question said, and the Hangman turned to him.

"Eh?"

"Sit down, old friend."

The Hangman sat then, not liking the way the Pastor's deep blue eyes rested on him, the way they peered out above his puffy red cheeks and thick black beard. They were somehow full of both sympathy and mischief at once. *Old friend*, he thought. *We ain't never been friends. Never in life, not even when you were just a grease monkey scamming folks for parts they didn't need.*

"Is there a problem, gentlemen?" the Hangman asked.

A great weight engulfed the bench beside him, the huge, hot mass of the Pastor, much too close for comfort. The Hangman didn't like the Pastor, not one bit. He stank of sweat and his breakfast sausage, and beneath that lingered the scent of grease and engine exhaust, like a stifling reminder that once upon a time this man's only religion came in the form of *god-damning* a sticky clutch or a bad carburetor.

"Bad times are coming, Hangman," the Pastor said with a sigh that sounded hokey and rehearsed.

"Bad times are already here, Pastor."

"Worse times. The interlopers draw nigh."

The Hangman fought to stifle a laugh. How much time had this imperious man studied the dictionary to find an antiquated phrase like that?

"They do," the Hangman continued. "Saw one out my car window on my way here."

"And no doubt you'll see more, maybe right up close and personal."

"They ain't never been much for—"

"There's a lot they ain't never been much for, Hangman," the Sheriff cut in. "Things change."

Things change. How very goddamn simplistic of him, this Sheriff who could watch two flies fuck all day while the world fell down around him. The Hangman didn't remember what the Sheriff had been before, but he was sure it wasn't any kind of lawman. He had simply been the first to strap on a gun, though he figured it took some measure of balls just to do that.

"The interlopers," the Pastor said, "will continue to grow bolder as they realize we are but simple creatures. Weak, slow, that this … *apocalypse* has left us vulnerable and far down on nature's food chain. What they need is appeasement, which we shall give."

"Appeas—Pastor, what exactly are you asking of me?"

The Pastor took a deep breath, steeling himself for his next words, but the Hangman new better. If anything could be said of the Pastor, it was that he was made of steel already.

He needed no tempering.

"We must make sacrifice, as the Lord once did with his only begotten son. We must show these creatures that we walk with God. We will give them an offering, our body and blood, the way the Savior did for us."

"But what—?"

"The body, Hangman," the Sheriff interjected. "You ain't gonna bury this one, nor any of them ever again, yer gonna leave them out for the—"

"That's fine, Sheriff," the Pastor said. "That's fine right there, thank you."

"Y-you want me to … *feed* our dead to these monsters?" the Hangman asked, his mouth going dry.

"We are not *feeding* them our dead, as you put it," the Pastor said. "We are making communion, both as an act of fealty and a way to show that we walk with the Lord."

"You can't be serious. Those things are animals, or—or … I don't know what. But they're not creatures of God that will follow His Law."

"*Every* creature is of God, my son," the Pastor said. "Large or small, *every* creature follows God's Law."

The Hangman could hardly believe how deluded this man was, but he supposed most religious were, even before the world had ended. The end of the world was really just an excuse for them to break out their finest china plates and sterling silver utensils to impress the dinner guests. The Hangman had never been impressed by such fineries. He believed God was the last hope of the poor and desperate, and such little hope He and His Holy Cronies provided in their constant absence and profound silence.

"Ain't no point in arguing, Hangman," the Sheriff chimed

in, "the decision has been made."

"By who?"

"By myself and the Pastor."

"And I spoke with God of this," the Pastor said. "This is His will. The decision was made by a much higher authority than ours."

"The decision to give them a taste for blood," the Hangman said. "For our flesh, after they've left us alone all this time?"

"We can have no idea what happens to the exiles once they step outside of our gates," the Pastor said.

"Right, so we may have been feeding them by accident for years. Now we're doing it on purpose." The Hangman was lost for a moment in the thought of those awful, bony jaws closing over flesh, those too-large teeth clamping down and tearing away, bones crunching and separating. He shuddered violently.

"And what exactly do you think keeps them off us when we're out here like we are now?" the Sheriff asked, any patience gone from his voice.

"Well I don't rightly know, Sheriff, they're animals. Could be the sound and stink of our diesels, the ruckus of our people, the shotguns your boys seem to so enjoy firing off for no goddamn reason except—"

"Now you hold on just a fuckin'—"

"Now now, boys," the Pastor said, as patient as ever. "We're talking ourselves in circles, and we've just about run out of time."

Sure enough, they could hear the diesel trucks on the gravel drive, the singing and laughing from the carriages. Not all of the townsfolk came for hangings, but most did.

People generally left their children at home; some didn't. There were no rules against children watching, but the Hangman thought it was tasteless and cruel. He'd never let his own children watch … except, of course, he would have to soon. His boy, now only fifteen, would soon have to learn his father's trade in order to ensure his own future. A legacy of death passed from father to son. His daughter would hopefully never see what they did out here on the hill.

The Sheriff turned to him, eyes slitted and mean the way they always were. "You got a goddamn job to do, Hangman. You gonna do it?"

"'Course I'm gonna do it," the Hangman replied, unable to keep the venom out of his own voice. "God help my soul, when have I ever *not* killed someone you brought me? I got more than enough blood on my hands, Sheriff, how 'bout you?"

The Sheriff made as if to grab him, but instead encountered the bulk of the Pastor in his way. It was one of the Pastor's great skills, to silently insinuate himself into any situation, simply allowing his great presence to hold power. It was, the Hangman thought, how he came to power in this town in the first place.

"Sheriff, if I could have you go out and make sure the congregation is properly seated and as calm as can be," the Pastor said, and the Hangman noticed the funny way the townsfolk became the 'congregation' automatically, regardless of how far from God this activity was. "The condemned will arrive soon, and we need these people to be as respectful as possible during this … very *difficult* execution."

The Sheriff glared at the Hangman, then his demeanor relaxed. He scratched his sunburned forehead, and in doing so unintentionally pushed his ridiculous straw hat back. In spite of his weasel face, he looked for a moment like Barney Fife, the incompetent, one-bullet toting deputy from *The Andy Griffith Show*, and the Hangman couldn't quite stifle a snicker. The Sheriff's eyes narrowed again, and Barney Fife was gone, replaced by a predatory animal.

"Laugh it up, Hangman. We'll see who's laughin' when you see whose neck's gettin' popped today."

"Go now, Sheriff, *please*," the Pastor said, for the first time sounding flustered, a sound that made the Hangman's stomach drop. He could have written off the Sheriff's comment as the man trying to get under his skin, but hearing the Pastor lose even a fraction of an ounce of control sent a cold chill of fear through him. In the wake of that tone, the Sheriff left quickly.

Who *was* he hanging this time? It had been bad enough watching Ms. Mina's head detach from her body, hearing her last grunt and cry, and then the sound of her flesh and bone separating at that vital seam. The rocks had hit the ground first, her little body following them, and then came the sound of blood running from the cavity where her head had been. And then, perhaps worst of all, the cheer of the crowd. How they loathed him, yet how they loved what he gave them.

"You're a Deist, my friend," the Pastor said.

"What?"

"You believe in God. You just think He doesn't care."

The Hangman thought about this for a moment. That was another power the Pastor had, the power to understand people, whether he liked them or not.

"I don't think He doesn't care on purpose, Pastor. I don't

think He's got time to care. I mean, look at us. If it's this bad here, imagine how bad it must be everywhere else. I reckon God's got His hands full."

The Pastor let out a low, soft rumble of a laugh. "How very wise of you. I believe you're wise enough, as well, to know that in God's absence, *or* His presence, His law must be followed."

God's laws, the Hangman thought, *or the laws humanity imposes on itself in God's name?* He said nothing of this, only let the Pastor get on his roll. The Hangman just wanted this day to be over with so he could go home and get smashed. Again. He had done it last night, and he'd do it again. He wasn't proud of it, though he wasn't ashamed, either. In these hoary last days of the world, filled with monsters and dust, it seemed fair for a man with a hard job—the hardest job—to embrace his alcoholism rather than reject it.

"Big or small," the Pastor continued, "young or old, God's laws reign over us all."

Young or old. The answer didn't require much imagination.

"So, it's to be another old-timer? Or … a *youngster*?" the Hangman asked, feeling the knot tighten in his stomach.

"A youngster, Hangman. Of reasonable age. Fifteen years or so, if I reckon properly. The child of … an important individual in this town."

The Hangman's head throbbed, his embattled blood vessels calling out their protest against his nightly drinking binges. Last night had been no exception, of course, and his only regret was how his family stayed away from him during those times. He hardly saw them at all. His grim, sour-faced wife darted through the house like a phantom.

His baby girl, only nine, generally played by herself outside in the dusty yard, and his boy....

"A young lady has turned up with child," the Pastor said, his voice growing soft and almost sympathetic. "Only thirteen years of age. *Thirteen*. Our youth is so dear and precious anymore that it's hardly fair for a girl of such an age to know the touch of a man, let alone to know the burden of motherhood. And the boy who would bring her to such a state...."

The Hangman could barely hear the rest over the song of his hangover, the song quickly becoming a *concert*. The math was simple, and yet he came to it slowly. And to think he had once been a math teacher; in those days, math, logic, and the deductive reasoning that could be performed with both had been a true joy in his life. The alcohol had slowed him significantly, he was sure—but no, he could not lay all the blame on just that. The *world* had slowed him significantly. *Death* had slowed him.

A fifteen-year-old boy.

A thirteen-year-old girl.

In what had once been a so-called civilized society, this combination would have still been reviled, and somehow celebrated at the same time. Teen parents, as he remembered, had been given television shows, media attention. There had been government assistance, food stamps, free healthcare. At the same time, men and women both had gone to prison all the time for having sexual relations with teenagers.

Daddy, I think I love her.

It had been a legal and moral dilemma in a place and time when the population was quickly overrunning the world. Even then, in more primitive parts of the world, teens had been coupled all the time. In primitive parts of the world where survival trumped every other aspect of the human condition. Just as it did now.

This ain't no time and place for love, he says, seeing the way his son pulls away from the sour puff of alcohol breath that follows his words.

Never, though, had he heard of a boy going to hang for sleeping with a girl only three years his junior. Until now. The rules, he knew, were different now, survival or not. This town was in the hands of men who would change the rules on a whim for their own purposes and get away with it. Every death was to be a message to the living. Who was *this* message for?

"Do you understand that this is true?" the Pastor asked. The Hangman no longer knew what he was talking about, had barely heard a word, and yet the question somehow made sense in the context of his thoughts.

"Who...," the Hangman began to ask, but trailed off, his mouth only wanting to form some kind of response to the Pastor's words. A part of him knew 'who' already, but the rest of him did not want to finish the thought. Might never finish the thought.

The Boy comes to him with stars in his eyes, and the Hangman's not so far gone yet that he can't see them. The Boy isn't prone to these kinds of looks; hardly anyone in this day and age is prone to this kind of whimsy anymore. It seems when the stars disappeared from the sky, they disappeared from people's souls as well. But the Boy has got them now, no doubt, and the Hangman isn't too far into his cups to notice.

'Whatchoo lookin' all gobsmacked for?' the Hangman asks

his son, hating the way the alcohol turns his words to mush. *This is why he mostly drinks alone.*

'Daddy, I think I love her.'

'This ain't no time and place for love,' he says, seeing the way his son pulls away from the sour puff of alcohol breath that follows his words.

'But I do!' The Boy's voice rises with childlike contention.

'You may think you do, but you're too young to know anything about love, real love.' The Hangman hates to see the way his boy's face drops, but when he's sloshed, he can't help the way he speaks. He thinks it's honesty, but knows it's also meanness. 'Especially here … there ain't no love left in this dry shithole of a world.'

'I love you,' the Boy says. 'And I love Momma and Sissy.'

The genuine truth in the Boy's words robs the Hangman of any further drunken retorts. The Boy still seems to sparkle with innocence, and teenage boys so rarely did that, even in the old world. The Hangman hates to see that sparkle die, and yet he knows it must eventually. This world will rob it from him like a thief in the night, and most likely the act will be violent.

The Hangman rose slowly from his bench like a man rising from the dead. He walked across the gravel road looping around Gallows Hill and began the slow, steady climb, foregoing the stairs and going straight up the steep side of the hill, his underused leg muscles burning almost immediately. He heard the Pastor behind him call out a question about putting his hood on, and he knew he should, but he didn't care. He had to see. He had to know the truth of the situation, to see the face of his latest victim, and if necessary, let his victim see the his face.

Laugh it up, Hangman. We'll see who's laughin' when you see whose neck's gettin' popped today.

A numb kind of dread spread through him, like the first roots of pure heartbreak being planted. It was the knowledge that all control was gone, that he could do nothing about what happened next. The knowledge that crying, screaming, and begging would be the order of the day, but that all of that spent energy would come to nothing, like trying to shout for water in the desert.

He made the top of the hill, his joints screaming. He should have put his hood on, yes, but that didn't matter because the audience—the congregation, the death-watch, whatever it could be called—was collectively turned away, watching as the mule-drawn cart carrying the condemned made its slow progress down Gallows Lane. The condemned had his hands tied behind his back and around a post that rose up from the back of the carriage. His legs were shaky and unstable, both from the bumpiness of the ride and from fear. He was blindfolded, and the blindfold wouldn't come off until he was atop the gallows. It would stay off while his execution order was read by the Sheriff, and then it would be replaced with a black hood if the condemned chose it. Then the rope.

A sound escaped the Hangman's lips that was part scream, part sob, part mad laughter, though where that came from and why it should be there, he had no idea. The combination of sound was despair.

"My boy, my boy, my boy," emerged from his lips in a harsh moan. He saw his future, his only hope for a future, approaching him in a cloud of dust, only to die by his own hand.

His eyes turned back and he searched the gathering desperately. At once, two heads turned back to him, their eyes filled with tears. One, his wife. The other, his little girl. She was nine years old, and if any boy dared to lay a hand on her, he'd kill him without hesitation. Did that, in this moment, make him the very worst kind of hypocrite?

You're a very pretty girl, he tells her.

She says, Thank you, and smiles.

His wife's eyes were full of black anger and exhaustion, and he thought he understood why. She must have dealt with all of this, the accusation, the 'trial,' the sentencing, while he was getting roaring drunk and then passing out at Lane Garrison's workshop the night before. And now that he thought about it, Lane himself had looked utterly stricken when he delivered the news that the Sheriff had come calling for a hanging. The Hangman had assumed it was simply the hangover. But had Lane known all along and been instructed not to tell? And if he did, would the Hangman ever be able to look at him square again?

His wife ... he could see the accusation in her eyes: If he had been home and sober, this might not have happened. Or at least she would have a partner in life to help carry this burden, which as it stood right now, she did not. She was to watch her drunk, absentee husband hang her beloved son. She must have known this from the moment the Sheriff or one of his deputies had come to fetch her for the trial. Her eyes burned into him for a few moments, and then turned away again. His little girl simply looked at him, confused and searching for answers. God help him, he had none.

He barely felt the hand fall on his shoulder; if he had,

his first instinct might have been to pull away. As it was, even through the numbness he could sense that godawful slab of meat resting on him, and he thought for a moment it might have been the last thing he'd ever feel in his life. He could only stand silently and stare at the vision of his boy, his only son, the condemned, being carted down Gallows Lane for his execution.

"You can't ask me to do this," the words tumbled from the Hangman's mouth.

"And yet I must. What he's done to that girl is an abomination in the eyes of God."

Sometimes, she says, when I fall asleep at night, I dream of havin' a sweet little baby all my own.

Girl like you's too young for such talk.

Am I?

"He spoke well for himself at the trial, Hangman," the Pastor continued. "You ought to be proud. He kept his head up like a man. He swears he has never been with that girl sexually. He claims … this is an immaculate conception. In many ways, he's strong with the Lord, and I truly believe that *he* believes what he says. But I believe we all know the truth."

Gray fingers crept into the corners of the Hangman's vision. It was his mind fighting against the truth and losing, his mind trying to inject every bit of denial it could possibly muster into this situation, and coming up short. He didn't feel the black executioner's hood slip out of his back pocket and appear in his trembling hand.

"Don your hood, Hangman, so they don't have to see the father hang his the son. It will be better that way, trust me. Do it quickly before they turn back around. They know who you are, but the hood allows them to disconnect your identity. Most of them."

"I—I can't."

"You must. Even the Lord God condemned His own son to die for the greater good."

"I ain't the Lord God," the Hangman said in a tremulous voice, "not even close. I can't! I *won't!*"

"That girl is pregnant at thirteen. It's as good as rape. She ain't saying much, but she did say it wasn't rape. But she's just a girl." The Pastor's eyes rested on him, and in that moment, the Hangman saw something in them. The truth.

He's drunk and alone in the house when the Girl comes calling for the Boy. The Boy isn't here, he tells her, but he invites her in for a drink of something cool after her long and fruitless walk. She accepts, and they talk a while. She's so pretty and young and vital, like his own Myra, only older, and becoming more like a woman. No, she is a woman, or so his wet brain tells him. She is drinking sweet tea; he is drinking Maker's Mark straight, and his brain is becoming wetter by the second. They talk about the Boy, and yes, she does love him, she says, and yes, he is still very innocent, he says, and she asks, doesn't he understand the world is moving on and there's barely enough time left for innocence, and he thinks this is an awfully adult thing for her to say, and he admires her for it. And wet brain or not, he also understands what she is saying.

'Sometimes,' she says, 'when I fall asleep at night, I dream of havin' a sweet little baby all my own.'

'Girl like you's too young for such talk.'

'Am I?'

'Yes.'

'I'd like a boy to kiss me sometime, that's all, and he won't even do that.'

'You're a very pretty girl,' he says.

She says, 'Thank you,' and smiles

He's well and truly drunk. And so he does what she wants. She doesn't exactly fight, but she doesn't exactly participate. She goes from being a woman to a girl and back again, over and over. And sometime in the midst of it, she is no longer a girl, just a vessel for what once was, his and his son's dreams all wrapped tightly together, and thrown into the heat of her fire.

The Hangman slowly and thoughtlessly drew the black hood over his head, as if to hide his face from himself. As if somehow the anonymity could make everything better.

"I was drunk," the Hangman said softly, allowing the hood to muffle him even more. The Pastor's eyes, still on him, narrowed slightly.

"Many people are well aware of your drinking habits, Hangman. Given your career path, I don't think anyone can blame you." The words were somehow forgiving and pitying and cold at the same time. The knife edge of truth still cut just beneath the Pastor's voice.

"I—I … sometimes I drink so much, I don't remember. I don't know sometimes … w-what I do."

"You ought be more careful with that sort of behavior, old friend. Suppose one day you were to do something you would regret. The consequences could be quite severe."

"I can't hang my boy, Pastor. He didn't do nothing wrong."

"Oh? Is there someone else you believe should be hanged today?"

The Pastor's eyebrows raised in mock curiosity, but those eyes still burrowed into him. The Hangman said nothing, could barely move. He wanted desperately to be sick, to be struck down in some way.

"Hangman? Is there? The condemned is but a few yards from the hill. Once he climbs the gallows, his fate is sealed. If you believe you can prove he is innocent, you must do so now."

Once again, the Hangman said nothing. He only stood and trembled and felt the hell of existence swirling around him uncontrollably.

"That girl will tell us nothing, Hangman. She only cradles that ridiculous bump in her young belly with a fool's grin on her face. She'll birth another baby into this cursed world, and there's nothing to be done about that. But the man—excuse me, the *boy*—that lay with her must pay the price. Will you do what must be done, Hangman, or will you stand there like a coward and simper?"

The Pastor's voice, though still low, was thunderous.

The Hangman's voice, so much smaller, so much weaker, said, "I can't."

"If you refuse to do your duty, if you are turned outcast into these wastes, who will take care of your family? Who will take care of *your* little girl? That pregnant girl had no father to speak for her, no father to protect her. Perhaps the next to be hanged will be the very transgressor who *rapes and impregnates your little girl.*" He finished with a huge clenched fist and eyes full of fire like the end of his most impassioned Sunday sermon, and the Hangman could see he had no choice.

"I—I ... I'll do what needs to be done, Pastor."

The Pastor's eyes softened and seemed to fill with a deep, soul-binding disappointment. *He was waiting for a confession*, the Hangman thought, *he* wanted *one. And didn't at the same time.*

"This world is damned," the Pastor said weakly. "Some days, I don't even know why I bother." Then he turned and gestured briskly to the Sheriff, who bound up the stairs to the gallows, removing his stupid straw hat and preparing to make his proclamation of execution.

The Pastor's hand clamped down hard around the Hangman's arm, so hard it was painful. The Hangman barely noticed. He'd wear the marks like a brand for a week.

"Get up there and do your goddamned job, *Hangman*." He shoved the Hangman away hard, and the smaller, older man almost stumbled and fell. Then he made his slow, weak-kneed way up the stairs of the gallows, where he stood beneath the structure he had built, and which he would use to kill his son in punishment for his own sins. *The sins of the Father*, he thought absently.

His eyes wandered across the horizon, where the clearing stopped and the forest began. He could see them there, just beyond the treeline. Those things that lived on the outside, the ones that would feed on his boy's body when all was said and done. He saw one emerge from the trees and shake its head like a lion, the mane of spikes and protrusions on its massive head clacked together in the process. That bony rattle was the worst part. And when all the townsfolk were gone from here, and the sun had dipped down closer to the horizon, those things would come out and drag his boy away. The Hangman shuddered violently.

The carriage stopped at the bottom of the hill. The matted,

skinny little mule that pulled it brayed loudly as if passing its own judgment.

"*Hear ye! Hear ye!*" the Sheriff announced, and the crowd immediately quieted. His words were still in his usual high tenor, but brisk and businesslike with a speech he had given many times. "We are gathered here to witness the execution of one James Trumbull, Jr., for the crime of rape and fornication, evidence heard, tried, and convicted by a jury of town elders. Should *any* man...," and here he paused, casting a weasely, sideways glance at the Hangman, "...wish to come forward with evidence against this conviction, he should do so now."

The silence was thunderous. The Hangman could hear only the beat of his heart, and he wished even that would stop. For a moment, he could feel his body stepping moving forward, his mouth calling out, *It was I, Sheriff. My boy is innocent. It was I who took advantage of that girl in a moment of weakness. It is my child she carries within her now. Spare the boy, and let me hang. I'll prepare the rope myself. Make it a good hang, make it messy, make it however you wish. I'll take the rope for my boy.*

But he said nothing.

"Very well," the Sheriff said. "Bring the condemned forward!"

The carriage driver untied the Boy's hands, helped him down, and tied his hands again in front of him. They made the long climb up the stairs to the top of the hill, then the shorter one to the top of the gallows. Once there, the Sheriff whipped the blindfold off the Boy's head. The Boy's eyes narrowed, blinked rapidly, watered, then slowly grew acclimated to the sudden flood of light. His face was red and scared, but the Hangman was proud to see he still held his head high as the Pastor had said. The Boy only faltered slightly when he looked at the hooded executioner.

"You got anything to say for yourself, Boy?" the Sheriff asked as a matter of course, but without much interest.

"No, Sir. I ain't done nothing wrong, but I'll take the rope anyway, if that's God's will."

"Very well. You are hereby sentenced to die by hanging. May God rest your soul."

The Sheriff glanced at the Hangman then as he stepped away, and damned if there wasn't the slightest smile on his face. Utter silence fell over the crowd, but in it, the Hangman swore he could hear his wife and daughter crying. He couldn't bring himself to look.

He stepped forward and put a hand on his boy's arm. It was still so soft, with a sheen of sweat on it. He remembered how soft it was when the boy was a baby, when he held the little man in his arms, the tiny squirming thing. His first true joy.

He pulled the boy gently to the trap and positioned him over it. He took down the rope, that deadly old friend, and checked the knot. It was true, tied well, and would do its job as always. It would be quick. He held it for a long time, and his boy watched him with a pair of glorious blue eyes, his body trembling slightly.

The Hangman removed his hood. The crowd gasped at this departure from ceremony, but the Boy's face lit a faint smile that touched the corners of his mouth.

"Hi, Daddy."

"My boy. My little Jimmy. I'm sorry."

"Don't be sorry, Daddy. I ain't scared. I never did nothing

wrong, I never laid a wrong finger on her, not once."

"I know, Boy, I—"

"She been touched by God, Daddy, don't you see?" The surety in his voice frightened the Hangman just a bit. Had the Boy gone mad in his last hours of life? "It's a virgin birth, jus' like in the Bible. She's carryin' the baby that'll save us all from this hell, you see?"

"Boy, this ain't—"

"I know what you're gonna say, Daddy, and it's okay. You ain't never much believed in God or the angels, and that's okay. They believe in you."

Did they, though? Would he ever be saved, even if it was all true? He didn't think so, not one bit.

"I'm ready to go, Daddy. I'm ready because I know that baby will make everything okay. You gotta look after her because I love her."

"I will, my boy."

The Boy was silent for a moment, looking at his father, his face stoic and strong. Then it softened, his mouth trembled a little, and his eyes filled with tears.

"Is it gonna hurt, Daddy?"

The Hangman finally looked at the noose in his hands. "Just for a second, son. Not long at all. I promise."

With that, the Boy's face hardened and the tears stopped welling in his eyes. The Hangman moved to place the noose over his head, then paused. How could he? How *could* he? To end his own son's life in such a manner, beneath such a vicious lie. To take him away from his mother, his sister, this world … this *world*….

It was that realization that steeled his resolve. It would be quick for his boy, and then nothing. The punishment for life did not come in the afterlife; it came in *life*. This life was the punishment for their sins, and after it was over … blessed rest. The townspeople didn't matter. Those things in the forest didn't matter. His boy would find peace one way or the other. He was a good boy, and he would find God.

"Do you want the hood, son?"

"No, Daddy. I ain't scared. And I wanna see you one last time. I'm sure glad it's you."

The Hangman placed the noose over his son's head. He tightened it just enough, placing the knot beneath the left side of the Boy's jaw. The Boy held his head high and didn't cringe or struggle like so many did. The Hangman was proud. He wished it was his own neck going into that noose. Maybe someday it would be. Maybe someday soon.

It was to be just the two of them now, the executioner and the condemned. The killer and the victim. The father and his son.

The Hangman stepped to the side and placed his hand on the wooden lever that would release the trap, the very lever he had made himself. He knew it better than almost anything else. It felt right in his hand.

The tears ran freely down his cheeks, and without his hood, everyone could see. They never knew that beneath his hood, he had cried for all of them.

"I love you, Daddy." Just loud enough for him to hear.

"I love you, Son. God bless you."

He pulled the lever.

The crack echoed across the barren land.

The Hangman's knot tightened.

Randolph's Room

Kaine Andrews

The silence is deafening. You've heard that before, I'm sure ... regardless of who "you" might turn out to be, it's a saying known the whole world around. People think it's a cliche, a bit of melodrama that horror hacks and drama nerds go berserk over. That may even be the truth. For most people.

But most people have never been in the room, either.

You might have seen it; some Facebook post or mentioned on Creepypasta. A room built to be perfectly soundless. An anechoic chamber, they call it. Lots of math and geometric gobbledegook behind it, but the idea is that there's no natural sounds in the construction. If nobody's in there, a tomb seems like a rowdy Spring Break in comparison.

They built them for sound effects purposes. To test audio qualities. To see what different species were capable of perceiving, without benefit of technology and without being hampered by ambient noise. All fine and well. Sometimes they even let tourists or students go in there and chill for a bit. But nobody lasted more than thirty minutes; too much of it, you start losing your grip.

All fine and well, until the government got their hands on it. They wanted to see if it'd work as some kind of torture device. Long story short, it did … but there were side effects they hadn't counted on. That "deafening silence" thing I mentioned first among them. The utter lack of sanity any of the subjects had after a day or two in there for another.

But there were compensations. They might have been crazy, but those subjects could hear a door opening a block and a half away. They could identify and transcribe a whisper heard two rooms over, if not further. Best part was, crazy as they were, they were controllable; a dog whistle would make them crumble, and all you had to do to keep them compliant was promise—in a whisper, of course; anything else and you'd rupture their eardrums—a half hour in the sensory deprivation tank. It was like heaven to them. It didn't stop them from hearing … but it brought it down to a tolerable level, if the interviews are to be believed.

How do I know all this? I was one of the government agents running this show. I took people—sometimes criminals, rapists and pederasts combed from the prison system, but just as often illegal immigrants or the homeless—and locked them in the room. Watched them for 24 to 48 hours. Let them out and observed.

Observation. That was my job description. I know better, now. It was torture.

Then came Randolph. Randy was black ops, or so the story goes. He might have known who killed Kennedy, who was really behind 9/11, what Snowden is really in trouble for. Or might have known if they weren't so busy keeping him doped up on a psychotropic cocktail and brainwashing him with a new identity and chain of memories every year or two. At least until he turned seventy, and the top brass decided they had a special place in mind for him.

Three years. That's how long they wanted us to lock him in the room. They didn't just want us to lock him down, though; they wanted the room altered. Normally, it's well lit. Temperature controlled, a nice sixty-five degrees. Humidity regulated at five percent (except on the occasions we had an asthmatic in there. Then they got generous and let us push it to 10%) and no air flow to disturb the "guests" or alter the sound levels.

That wasn't enough. The biggies wanted the lights killed. Zero light penetration. They wanted the temp cut back to fifty, wanted the humidity rolled back to only two percent. Wanted nerve-deadeners and muscle relaxants dropped in the rations.

They wanted to completely kill any sensation; they figured if dropping hearing for a few days was enough to turn people into dogs, dropping *everything* for an extended period would result in some kind of superhuman senses.

We did it. God help us, we did it. We went along when they started pumping white noise into the room at random intervals. Went along when they started hiding subliminal messages under that. We handed over every scrap of paper Randy scribbled on—nothing for the first few months, but he started getting pretty prolific for a while there; when he stopped writing six days ago, I probably should have noticed something was wrong—without looking at them.

Knowing what I do now, I don't know how he held on so long. I don't know how he managed to write those notes, day after day for over two years. I can't begin to grasp how he survived the broadcasts; from my side of the glass, they were just faint hints of static, there and then gone. From his, it must have sounded like an avalanche.

How do I know? I'll tell you, in a minute. But first I have to finish telling you about Randy. Then you'll understand.

He went mad; of course he did. But he was quiet. He screamed for the first two days straight. By the third, his voice had given out. By the fourth, he'd started to adjust, and was making every attempt to make as little noise as possible. All expected reactions. Then we turned out the lights. When we'd let him out, to take him to sens-dep or quiz him, we had to open the door a crack and throw him a pair of sunglasses. Otherwise his eyes would start bleeding, prompting screaming, which would rupture his eardrums.

We learned quick. Too quick.

His eyes lost all coloration; they were nothing but pupils the last time I saw them, and I still bet he didn't see much. At least not the way we understand it. That was part of it, too; the government was getting their perfect little pet psychic, all right ... but we didn't know it until it was too late. And there's always the matter of cost. The cost is just too high. All of us are going to Hell for what we've done, what we've *allowed* to be done.

Three days ago, we came for him; he hadn't written, hadn't whispered back to the discreet speakers that broadcast the white noise, hadn't moved in 72 hours; we thought he was dead. I went in first, cracking the door and tossing his sunglasses in—which was all but guaranteed to provoke a reaction, as even the imperceptible click of the rubber frames against the padded and insulated floor was enough to set him off anymore—but got no reaction. Daring further, I gestured for the doctor and my attendant to hang back, and stepped into the room.

That was a mistake. I only got a glimpse of him, but he told me the rest later; all I could see was that his eyes were gone, empty sockets dripping blood and the tattered remnants of the optic nerve. He jumped at me, shoved me aside, and dove for the door.

The door swung shut behind him. I didn't know how or why at the time; it should have been impossible. It opened into the room, was six feet wide and eight feet tall, made of padded steel and locked with a valve mechanism. As emaciated as he was it would have taken Randy a lot of effort to pull it shut, let alone lock it, but by the time I hit it and attempted to open it, it was already locked.

I raised my fist to bash on the door, knowing that Randy was probably down in the hall, either shot by my assistant or tranq'd by the doc, but as I went to bring my hand down, I froze. Every nerve in my body was suddenly on fire, my throat was closing and despite the utter darkness I could *see*. I could see what was happening outside; Randolph was just standing there, smiling. The doc was shoving his hypodermic into his own neck, shoving the plunger down all the way and delivering what was almost certainly a fatal dose of flupenthixol direct to his brain. My second had his pistol drawn, seemed about ready to kneecap Randolph ... then turned the gun to his own temple and pulled the trigger. I heard laughter, and knew it belonged to Randy; high and strange, it seemed to carry much worse than psychotic mirth. I found my own mouth opening and I began to laugh along.

Through the laughter, Randy spoke to me. Told me what we'd really made.

"I'm deaf, now. But I hear *everything*," he said, and I saw him raise a pencil—the one I'm writing this with, in fact—to his ear and shove it in before repeating the task on the other side. He didn't need his ears anymore, you see. They were a hindrance, the frequency his own eardrums made in the complete absence of sound worsening his madness and prompting migraines.

"I may be blind. But I can see *everything*," he told me. The image of the hall, what befell my fellow researchers? The images that followed, where he murdered everyone in the building? All of them were what he was seeing, watching it all like a spectator lurking just behind him ... but that wasn't all he saw. He showed me things from the brass' office in D.C.; showed me a child dying in a gutter somewhere south of the Sahara; showed my ex-wife and her new lover, fucking like rabid wolves on the bed I'd picked out, in the house my government contracts had bought. He saw everything; he showed me everything. He showed me how he gouged out his own eyes, tired of looking through them while watching himself, tired of hearing them swivel in their sockets like trapped gerbils, tired of the sound of his own blinking.

"I can't feel anything ... but I can feel *everything*. And feeling it is the first step to controlling it." That was the last thing he said to me. To prove it, he made me dance. I drug myself to my feet and did the worst Riverdance imperson-ation anyone's ever seen; he made me do the splits, tearing a few muscles in my thighs in the process. He made me weep, made my eyes feel as though they'd been filled with acid, then made me resume laughing uncontrollably. He did worse, but it doesn't really matter. Between that and what he'd done in the hallway, I knew his control was total, if he wanted it to be.

We made a monster. A mad God that knows only some-one hurt him—badly—and wants revenge. One who has seen every instance of pain, suffering, and lust both as himself and as every human on the face of the earth, and isn't going to take it anymore. In depriving him of all the things that make us human, we made him something else … and now he's loose.

Nobody is coming for me. I accept that. I could wait—the automatic systems will keep delivering food packets and water until the generators die, and that will take years—but I'm already losing my grip. Already starting to understand what we really did to him.

I've been in here for three days. He was in here for three years. He showed me some of what he's become, but I refuse to allow that to happen to me; what's already happening is bad enough. The sound of this pencil rubbing lead against this notepad is maddening. My head is throbbing, and despite the lack of light every pulse of my brain brings with it a flash of the paper in front of me, a view of myself from over my own shoulder. I don't know why it's taking me so quickly, but I think Randy did something to me, broke something inside that would have let me resist this longer.

I won't be like him. I can't. When I'm done, I'm going

to do what he did; dig this pencil into my ear. But I won't stop at the eardrum. I'm going to shove it through. All the way. Suicide may be a mortal sin, but I think I've committed enough of those already; won't make much difference. If there was a surer way, I'd take it, but I left my gun on my desk—in case you have to go into the room, it's always best to avoid temptation—and there's nothing to hang myself from in here.

The silence is deafening. I understand that, now. When it's so quiet you can literally hear your blood flowing through you, when a pencil on paper sounds like dogs clawing at the backdoor for a 3 am potty break, when even blinking carries with it the sound of a gunshot ... then you'd understand. When it's so quiet that your thoughts start to seem like a heavy metal concert beside your ear, instead of whispers in the back of your head ... now you're getting there.

The silence is deafening. It's time to go.

CONTRIBUTORS

A 29-year-old living in the Twin Cities with his wife and son, *Troy Blackford* has sixteen published short stories and an audiobook short story collection out through In Ear Entertainment. His stories have been featured in places like *Bewildering Stories, Inkspill Magazine, Roadside Fiction, The Glass Coin*, and the '*Over My Dead Body!' Mystery Magazine*. His website is **http://www. troyblackford.com**.

D.W. Gillespie is a longtime horror writer and fan who lives in middle Tennessee. When he's not at his day job, he spends most of his time wrangling his two young children, two dogs, and two cats. Most of his nights are spent lying in bed and dreaming up awful, twisted things to write about. These stories, in turn, are read by his loving wife who immediately wonders whether or not she is sharing a bed with a crazy person. Follow D.W. on facebook at **https://www.facebook.com/dw.gillespie**.

James Michael Shoberg has many years of diverse experience in theatre. He is an award-winning actor and playwright, as well as a designer and director. His writing credits include numerous fringe plays and monologues. James is also the Co-Executive Producer/Artistic Director/Resident Playwright of The Rage of the Stage Players fringe theatre company in Pittsburgh, Pennsylvania, now entering its thirteenth season.

In 2011, he acquired the permission of the filmmakers known as The Butcher Brothers, and Lionsgate Films, to write, produce, and direct a world-premiere stage adaptation of their award-winning independent horror film, *The Hamiltons*, for The Rage of the Stage Players. In October 2013, they will premiere his next play, a steampunk stage adaptation of Oscar Wilde's, *The Picture of Dorian Gray*. James' unusual brand of twisted theatre has already attracted attention both nationally and internationally, and he is always seeking new venues for future productions of his work.

Adam Millard is the author of thirteen novels and more than a hundred short stories, which can be found in various collections and anthologies. Probably best known for his post-apocalyptic fiction, Adam also writes fantasy/horror for children. He created the character Peter Crombie, Teenage Zombie just so he had something decent to read to his son at bedtime.

Adam also writes Bizarro fiction for several publishers, who enjoy his tales of flesh-eating clown-beetles and rabies-infected derrieres so much that they keep printing them. His "Dead" series has been the filling in a Stephen King/Bram Stoker sandwich on Amazon's bestsellers chart, and the translation rights have recently sold to German publisher, Voodoo Press. Adam also writes for *This Is Horror*, whose columnists include Shaun Hutson, Simon Bestwick, and Simon Marshall-Jones. Adam lives in the post-apocalyptic landscape known as Wolverhampton, England, with his wife, Zoe, and son, Phoenix.

Melissa Ferguson is the author of over fifteen published short stories and creative non-fiction works. Her story *Sergiane's Choice* was adapted from a novel called *Dandelion Island* that came to life during NaNoWriMo 2012. She works as a cancer-fighting scientist and is undertaking a Masters in Human Nutrition. She writes when her children are pretending to be asleep.

The authors that currently inspire her include; Margo Lanagan, Peter V Brett, Max Brooks and Robin McKinley. Her all-time favourite book is *The Day of the Triffids* by John Wyndham. For NaNoWriMo 2013 Melissa intends to write about a cloned Neanderthal girl. She can be found on the couch reading a book in Geelong, Australia or at **storiesbymelissa.tumblr.com**.

Brent Abell resides in Southern Indiana with his wife, sons, and a pug who thinks he rules all mankind. He works full time, but has found time to be published in or have tales coming out from multiple presses and eZines. *In Memoriam*, his debut novella, was released in October 2012 from Rymfire Books. You can hang out with him for some rum, a cigar, and all the latest news at **http://brentabell.wordpress.com**.

O.D. Hegre is a former academic, teaching and involved in biomedical research at the University of Minnesota and later in the biotech industry. After three decades plus of trying to understand how the world worked, he retired. Now Orie sits at his keyboard everyday, spending less time thinking about how things really are and more time imagining how they could be.

Marc Sorondo lives with his wife and children in New York. He loves to read, and his interests range from fiction to comic books, physics to history, oceanography to cryptozoology, and just about everything in between. He's a long time student and occasional teacher. For more information, go to **MarcSorondo.com**.

Sean Moreland is an editor, teacher, and writer. He has published about two-dozen poems and a handful of short stories, mainly in independent Canadian periodicals. He is founder and a fiction editor of *Postscripts to Darkness*, a serial anthology of weird fiction and art. He has a Ph.D. in English from the University of Ottawa, where he currently teaches part-time.

On the academic side of things, he co-edited the essay collection *Fear and Learning: Essays on the Pedagogy of Horror* (McFarland, 2013), is in the early stages of co-editing *Holy Terrors: Essays on Monstrous Children in Cinema*, and has recently published chapters in a number of books, including *Deciphering Poe* and *Generation Zombie*. You can find out more about him, or *Postscripts to Darkness*, by going to **www.pstdarkness.com**, following **@pstdarkness** on Twitter, or by hunting him down on Facebook.

Brandon Ketchum is a freelance writer working in the fantasy, horror, and science fiction genre. His preferred sub-genres to write include dark and weird horror and fantasy, combined science fiction and fantasy, and urban fantasy. He has been published in *Mad Scientist Journal, Innsmouth Free Press* and *Schlock! Webzine*. Brandon recently attended the Cascade Writers' Workshop.

Mason Gall is an aficionado of fine whiskey and sometimes writer living in Asheville, North Carolina. He has several published short stories, and one published novel currently out of print due to its morally challenging themes. Mason does not network socially, but can be reached for no-comment at **masongall81@gmail.com**.

Kaine Andrews was born in San Diego, California, before being spirited away to Carson City, Nevada. There he has remained, with the exception of one memorable week in Bend, Oregon and one small tour in hell (AKA Chandler, Arizona.)

Raised among a family filled with NASCAR loving, mechanically minded folk who considered themselves witches, Kaine's unique upbringing and early escape from the halls of education, along with the theft of his father's typewriter, led him to the demented scribbling that he refers to as his "work."

Through the course of his life, Kaine has been involved in television production, retail work, criminal psychology, newspaper writing, radio, and criminology as well as earning trade-school degrees in private investigation, computer programming, freelance writing, and motorcycle repair. This eclectic background has left him with a fractured worldview and a number of unique experiences to translate into his writing.

He currently remains in Carson City, while dreaming of the Oregon coast, wrestling with his pet coyote, and hoping to one day elope with Katy Perry.

Logan Knight (cover artist), AKA, KnightmanProductions has been creating some form of art since early in life, but in 1997 Logan began his journey into creative freedom ... during the next several years he created an online presence that has allowed him to share his art in various forms.

Logan is a prolific artist who does not believe in creative limits, always willing to try new things; his art continues to progress into areas of surreal, dark fantasy, abstract digital, & colorful fractal art. Logan has created art for cell phones, worked with Sony Ericsson offering exclusive art for their phones, as well as offering several hundred images for download through his work with www.Arphiola.com.

His artwork has also been used for several independent bands' CD covers, book covers, website art, and much more. You can see more of his work and contact him for commissioned art at:
www.knightmanproductions.com.

ADVERTISING

At Pavor Nocturnus and Parasomnia Press, we believe that all independent artists—those brave souls out there in the world doing the work they love without the guarantee of the big money we would all so love—deserve as much promotion as they can get. The work is hard enough, and frequently expensive. Why should any hard-working indie artist have to break the bank to get a little promotion when there are so many of us doing the very same thing, and on shoestring budgets?

We're proud to offer free advertising to our contributors, staff, and creative partners, and to offer extremely low rates for everyone else. If you're interested in advertising with us, please contact us at **advertising@pavnoc.com**. We'll be happy to negotiate rates with you, and if you can't afford a designer to put together your ad? Well, we'll throw that in as well. For the same price. We do the work because we love the work, and we want to do all we can to help *your* work get seen without bleeding your cash reserves dry.

So shoot us an e-mail and see how we can work with you. In return, please visit and support our advertisers! All of us need as much creative love as we can get.

I promise
This won't hurt one bit.

A new voice in literary horror
pstdarkness.com

Disciple of Grief

Raine Andrews

Book I of The Disciples
Previously published as "Darkness of the Soul"

Pavor Nocturnus Dark Fiction Anthology
is a publication of Parasomnia Press.

Please visit us online at:

www.pavnoc.com
facebook.com/pavnoc
@pavnocdfa

All submissions are accepted at:

https://pavnoc.submittable.com/submit

See our website for submissions guidelines.

www.parasomniapress.com

www.ingramcontent.com/pod-product-compliance
Lightning Source LLC
Chambersburg PA
CBHW071245130626
46556CB00003B/1178